PENGUIN CLASSICS

FABLES OF AESOP

Aesop probably lived in the middle part of the sixth century B.C. A statement in Herodotus gives ground for thinking that he was a slave belonging to a citizen of Samos called Iadmon. Legend says that he was ugly and misshapen. There are many references to Aesop found in the Athenian writers: Aristophanes, Xenophon, Plato, Artistotle and others. It is not known whether he wrote down his Fables himself, nor indeed how many of them are correctly attributed to his invention.

•

S. A. Handford was born at Manchester in 1898 and educated at Bradford Grammar School and at Balliol College, Oxford, where he took a 'double first' in classics. He was a lecturer in Swansea, and Lecturer and Reader at King's College, London. He published several books on classical subjects, and translated Caesar's *The Conquest of Gaul*, Sallust's *The Jugurthine War* and *The Conspiracy of Cataline* (in one volume) and Aesop's *Fables* for the Penguin Classics, besides revising the present volume. He died in October 1978.

¶ FABLES OF AESOP

TRANSLATED BY S. A. HANDFORD

WITH ILLUSTRATIONS BY

BRIAN ROBB

PENGUIN BOOKS

PENGUIN BOOKS

Published by the Penguin Group
Penguin Books Ltd, 27 Wrights Lane, London W8 5TZ, England
Viking Penguin, a division of Penguin Books USA Inc.
375 Hudson Street, New York, New York 10014, USA
Penguin Books Australia Ltd, Ringwood, Victoria, Australia
Penguin Books Canada Ltd, 2801 John Street, Markham, Ontario, Canada L3R 1B4
Penguin Books (NZ) Ltd, 182–190 Wairau Road, Auckland 10, New Zealand

Penguin Books Ltd, Registered Offices: Harmondsworth, Middlesex, England

This translation first published 1954
New edition 1964
21 23 25 27 29 30 28 26 24 22

Copyright 1954 by S. A. Handford
All rights reserved

Printed in England by Clays Ltd, St Ives plc
Set in Monotype Poliphilus

¶ Contents

INTRODUCTION

TRANSLATION

¶ Introduction

I. THE FABLE IN GREECE BEFORE AESOP

Popular stories of one sort and another have existed in every place and age; and since primitive man has usually lived in close contact with wild and domestic animals, it was natural for him to invent stories describing imaginary adventures of animals and to make them act and speak with motives and emotions proper to human beings. The special characteristic of the fable is that it is designed, or can easily be adapted, to teach a lesson in morality or prudence. In a good fable the lesson is implicit in the narrative itself, so that he who runs may read it; but in course of time most fables were provided with a 'moral' – an explicit statement of the teaching which they were intended to convey. This method of imparting simple instruction for the wise conduct of life is ingenious, striking, and effective. It has so caught men's fancy that many peoples have a corpus of fables either adapted from or modelled on some of those which have been in existence for centuries.

There are no fables in the Homeric poems, but a few occur in Greek poetry as early as the eighth or seventh century B.C. The Boeotian poet Hesiod* narrates a story of a hawk and a night-ingale (compare No. 73 in this selection). The fragments of Archilochus,† a poet of the island of Paros, contain parts of at least two fables – that of the eagle and the vixen (No. 67 below), and one about a fox and a monkey (perhaps similar to No. 5). These poems are several centuries earlier than the earliest known fables of any other country. A collection of Indian fables, which was formerly supposed to have been a model for Greek fables, is now known to contain nothing earlier than the fourth century, and most of it is probably of much later origin. Moreover, the parallelism between the

* *Works and Days*, 202–12.   † Frag. 89 ff., 81 ff. (Diehl).

Greek and the Indian fables is rarely close enough to suggest direct dependence. There is reason to believe that some Egyptian and Assyrian fables became known to the Greeks in classical times, but no evidence exists to suggest that these influences were either early or important. As far as we can see, therefore, the fable was invented by the Greeks – it may well be, by the Greeks of Asia Minor, the country of the lion which appears so often in these stories, and the traditional birthplace of Aesop.

2. AESOP

By the latter part of the fifth century, Aesop (Aisōpos) had become a familiar name in Greece and he was commonly spoken of not merely as *an* author, but as *the* author, of fables. We possess very little certain information about him, and it has even been held that no such person ever lived, and that the name represents nothing more than an imaginary inventor of the fable – for the Greeks liked to ascribe each kind of composition to a real or fictitious 'finder out'. There is, however, early and reliable authority for the actual existence of Aesop in the *Histories* of Herodotus,* who, writing in the second half of the fifth century, (1) states that Aesop the maker of stories lived in the time of the Egyptian pharaoh Amasis (i.e. the middle of the sixth century) and was connected with the island of Samos; (2) gives reason for thinking that he was a slave belonging to a Samian citizen called Iadmon; (3) implies that Aesop met his death at the hands of the people of Delphi. Herodotus speaks of him as a well-known person and assumes that the place and manner of his death are common knowledge; and there is no reason for doubting the truth of what he says. As to Aesop's being a slave, the position is not quite clear. Herodotus gives good cause for believing that, if he was a slave, he was a slave of the Samian Iadmon; but he does not

* II 134.

tell us how he knows that Aesop was a slave at all, and the evidence which he adduces would be consistent with his being not a slave but a relative of Iadmon. However, his servile condition was universally accepted in antiquity, and it may well have been an established fact, too well known to need any proof.

The statements of later writers about Aesop must be accepted with caution, because we generally have no means of knowing whether they rest on good authority. They tell us that he was by birth a Phrygian (or a Thracian), and they give more or less circumstantial accounts of his death. Aristophanes* says the Delphians accused him of stealing a cup from their temple. Plutarch† says that he gave offence to the Delphians, who in revenge trumped up a charge of sacrilege against him and put him to death by hurling him from a rock. A commentator on Aristophanes adds a further detail: they 'planted' a gold cup belonging to the temple in Aesop's baggage – a story suspiciously like other stories, such as that of Joseph and Benjamin in *Genesis*. Eventually his name became the centre of fantastic legends. He was alleged to have been a preternaturally ugly, misshapen little man, whose hideous appearance contrasted strikingly with his brilliant sallies of wisdom. He made everyone laugh not only by the cleverness of his story-telling but by his grotesque manner and his stammering speech. Finally, after he died he came back to life and fought at the battle of Thermopylae!

From the fifth century onwards the Aesopian fable and the tradition of Aesop the story-teller became very popular, especially at Athens, as is shown by many references to him or to fables attributed to him – in Aristophanes, Xenophon, Plato, Aristotle, and other writers. We do not know whether Aesop's own versions of any fables were written down by him or by any of his contemporaries; and even supposing that some of them were written, it is very unlikely that they are preserved in the versions that we possess. It is clear that Aesop's name

* *Wasps*, 1446–7.   † *De sera numinis vindicta*, 12.

was so closely associated with this kind of story that *any* fable came to be spoken of as a fable of Aesop. Aristophanes* attributes to Aesop the fable of the eagle and the vixen which was known to Archilochus a century and a half before Aesop's time, and it appears later in collections of 'Fables of Aesop'.

3. LATER HISTORY OF THE FABLE

After Aesop's lifetime, newly invented fables were nearly always attributed to him. Most of them, old and new, would certainly be current in different forms, expanded or abridged, and would be continually varied in the detail. There is evidence that, before the beginning of the Christian era, the adaptation or invention of fables became a regular part of a rhetorical training.

The earliest recorded collection was made at Athens about 300 B.C., but nothing is known about it beyond the fact that it was compiled by Demetrius, a famous citizen of the Attic deme of Phalerum. A few fables occur in Greek and Latin literature of the second and first centuries. Horace alludes to several and narrates or summarizes three (see the notes to Nos. 1, 41, 46). A collection which is probably the earliest now extant was made in Latin verse by Phaedrus, a slave born in Macedonia who lived most of his life at Rome and became a freedman of the emperor Augustus. It includes many fables of which we have also Greek versions; others which, though not elsewhere known, are doubtless of Greek origin; and some – clearly Phaedrus' own invention – which refer to contemporary social and political conditions. Most of these stories are simply and concisely told in language made attractive by its liveliness and charm.

Several Greek authors of the first and second centuries A.D. introduce fables into their works – a few of them apparently new, but for the most part known to us from other sources. A

* *Birds*, 651–3.

good many are narrated or referred to in the biographies and moral treatises of Plutarch, and in the satirical dialogues and romances of Lucian. The first extant Greek collection of known authorship was made by Babrius, a hellenized Roman who, not later than the end of the second century, wrote some 140 versions in verse. There is some artificiality in his treatment of the stories, and his style shows the affection and debasement which characterize much of the Greek literature of the period, when Greek had become a cosmopolitan language. But he had literary skill and caught the ear of his contemporaries. Some of his fables are not otherwise known to us, but these may well be derived from earlier collections of which no record has been preserved.

About A.D. 400 the Roman Avianus composed forty-two fables in Latin verse, using Babrius as his main source and expanding his originals by the addition of much descriptive detail. It is sad stuff, but commentaries on and quotations from his text show that it long remained popular.

Prose paraphrases of the poems of Phaedrus and Avianus began to be made from the fifth century onwards, and it was chiefly through the medium of these that later centuries – when neither the Greek versions nor, it may be, Phaedrus and Avianus themselves, were much read – obtained their knowledge of fables. A collection of French versions appeared as early as the tenth century and was followed by many others, culminating in the seventeenth century with the masterpiece of Jean de la Fontaine. Isolated fables occur in English literature from the earliest times and there are collections dating from the fifteenth century. All these French and English collections, though they may contain a certain amount of original matter, are based mainly on traditional stories descended ultimately from classical Greek sources.

In addition to the metrical versions mentioned above – of limited scope, but of known authorship – we possess much more comprehensive collections in Greek prose of unknown authorship and date. These are preserved in more than forty manuscripts, containing between them over 350 fables. The collections vary greatly in size and content. Some fables are recorded in only one or two manuscripts; others appear in many manuscripts, which sometimes give several differing versions of the same tale.

Apart from those fables which are narrated or referred to by authors of known date – Aristophanes, Horace, Phaedrus, Plutarch, Babrius, and others – there is no external evidence to show when most of these stories were first invented; and we can only try to guess when some of them were cast into their present form. Some scholars have believed that almost all our anonymous versions were written at a very late date, not before the ninth century A.D. Two facts seem to lend some support to this view. First, a few versions have 'morals' appended to them which were obviously written by Christians who knew their Bible (see, for example, Nos. 81, 197); secondly, some versions contain Greek words of very late date. This opinion, however, was strongly controverted by Emile Chambry.* In answer to the arguments mentioned above, he points out that

(1) Each of the 'morals' in question appears in only one or two manuscripts, the same fables being given in other manuscripts with 'morals' which may date from the pagan era;

(2) The Christian 'morals' may very well have been added to or substituted for other 'morals' at a later date than the versions of the fables themselves were composed;†

* See pp. xlii–xlvii of his introduction.

† Most of the ' morals ' attached to the fables of Avianus are clearly of medieval date, although Avianus wrote about the year 400.

(3) Both the Christian 'morals' and the really late Greek words are very few in number, and are completely absent from one whole group of manuscripts – which makes it probable that there was a well-established text of the pieces contained in these manuscripts, handed down from a period either before or not long after the beginning of the Christian era.

Chambry justly claimed that this is confirmed by the language and style of a number of the fables, which are typically classical in their clarity, simplicity, naturalness, and freedom from all affectation. He thought that the earliest of the extant collections was formed round a nucleus of versions going back well into pre-Christian times; and most modern scholars would agree that it was probably made at any rate by the end of the second century A.D. Many of the other collections preserved in our manuscripts certainly contain material which is both very much later – some of it written not before the fifth century, and perhaps a good deal later – and of very much poorer quality. Even some of the good stories are told in a flat and commonplace style and there are many pieces (not included in the present selection) so jejune or puerile that they scarcely merit attention.

5. SUBJECT-MATTER OF THE FABLES

Nearly three-quarters of the extant fables are stories about animals, and there can be no doubt that this was the original and always the most popular type. Only a few are concerned with plants or natural elements such as the sea, rivers, the sun, and the winds. There are, however, a good many in which the actors are gods or men, or both gods and men. Several of these are aetiological – *How the Tortoise got its Shell* (No. 64), *Why the Ant is a Thief* (No. 136), *Why Giants are Boobies* (No. 153), and the like. Most of the rest are merely anecdotes, often concluding with a *bon mot* of some kind, and generally capable of being used as a peg on which to hang a moral lesson or a piece of advice. These epilogues soon came to be regarded as an essential element, and if a story did not lend itself to the purpose, some sort of 'moral' was nevertheless plastered on to it, even if it had to be attached to some comparatively unimportant detail of the anecdote.

Since the fable is essentially a popular *genre* of literature, it naturally reflects the ideas of ordinary people about the conduct of life. It has little to do with the ideals of virtue and the pursuit of perfection inculcated by the great ethical philosophers of antiquity. The virtues recommended by the fabulists are chiefly the social virtues which make life comfortable and redound to the credit and interest of those who practice them – loyalty, gratitude, moderation, resignation, industry, and so on. Sometimes the lessons they teach are not really moral lessons at all, but merely counsels of prudence and wordly wisdom based on observation of people's behaviour and degenerating at times into frank *im*morality – how to get the better of an enemy (or even of a friend), how to keep a whole skin by subservience to the possessors of power, how to profit by other men's misfortunes and mistakes, and in general how to turn everything to good account for oneself.

6. PRONUNCIATION OF PROPER NAMES

In the list of proper names on the opposite page the accent ' is placed after the syllable which has the stress. All long vowels (ā) are marked; short vowels (ă) are marked only when it is desired to call special attention to them. It should be noted that *eu* is a diphthong, not two separate vowels.

Aenē′ās   Dēmē′trius   Menē′nius
Alcmē′nē   Dēmos′thenēs   Mŏ′mus
Amphi′tryōn   Diony̆′sus   Mycē′nae
Anchi′sēs   Eleu′sis   Persĕ′phŏnē
Aphrodī′tē   (three syllables)   Phalē′rum
Archi′lochus   E′phesus   Pīrae′us
Aristo′phanēs   Eurys′theus   Plū′tus
A′ristŏtle   (three syllables)   Promē′theus
Ar′temis   Hēphaes′tus   (three syllables)
Athē′nā   Hē′rā   Sējā′nus
Aviā′nus   Hē′raclēs   Sū′nium
Cali′gula   Her′mēs   Thermŏ′py̆lae
Dē′los   Hē′siod   Xe′nophōn
Del′phī   Kŏ′rē   Zeus
Dēmā′dēs   Lē′thē   (monosyllable)
Dēmē′tēr   Lē′tō

NOTE

Three critical editions of the fables have been published in the last forty years: (1) É. Chambry: *Aesopi Fabulae* (Paris, 1925–6); the text of the best versions was reprinted, with a French translation, in the 'Budé' series (Paris, 1927); (2) B. E. Perry: *Aesopica,* Vol. I (Univ. of Illinois Press, Urbana, 1952), containing an excellent text of the earliest version of each fable; (3) A. Hausrath: *Corpus Fabularum Aesopicarum* (Teubner, Leipzig, 1956–9). There is also an older edition in the Teubner series, by C. Halm (1852). The present selection includes some fables translated from the Latin of Phaedrus (text by J. P. Postgate in Oxford Classical Texts; by J. Gow in Postgate's *Corpus Poetarum Latinorum*; text with French translation by A. Brenot in the 'Budé' series).

Fables of Aesop

A CASE FOR PATIENCE

A half-starved fox, who saw in the hollow of an oak-tree some bread and meat left there by shepherds, crept in and ate it. With his stomach distended he could not get out again. Another fox, passing by and hearing his cries and lamentations, came up and asked what was the matter. On being told, he said: 'Well, stay there till you are as thin as you were when you went in; then you'll get out quite easily.'

¶ This tale shows how time solves difficult problems.

A fox slipped in climbing a fence. To save himself from falling he clutched at a brier-bush. The thorns made his paws bleed, and in his pain he cried out: 'Oh dear! I turned to you for help and you have made me worse off than I was before.' 'Yes, my friend!' said the brier. 'You made a bad mistake when you tried to lay hold of me. I lay hold of everyone myself.'

¶ The incident illustrates the folly of those who run for aid to people whose nature it is to hurt rather than to help.

SOUR GRAPES

A hungry fox tried to reach some clusters of grapes which he saw hanging from a vine trained on a tree, but they were too high. So he went off and comforted himself by saying: 'They weren't ripe anyhow.'

¶ In the same way some men, when they fail through their own incapacity, blame circumstances.

4
ACTIONS SPEAK LOUDER
THAN WORDS

A fox was being chased by huntsmen and begged a wood-cutter whom he saw to hide him. The man told him to go into his hut. Soon afterwards the huntsmen arrived and asked if he had seen a fox pass that way. He answered 'No' – but as he spoke he jerked a thumb towards the place where the fox was hidden. However they believed his statement and did not take the hint. When the fox saw they had gone he came out and made off without speaking. The woodman reproached him for not even saying a word of acknow-ledgement for his deliverance. 'I would have thanked you,' the fox called back, 'if your actions and your character agreed with your words.'

¶ This fable is aimed at men who make public profession of virtue but behave like rogues.

FOOLS DIE FOR WANT OF WISDOM

A monkey made a great impression by dancing before an assembly of animals, who elected him their king. The fox was jealous. Noticing a snare with a piece of meat in it, he took the monkey to it and said: 'Here is a choice titbit that I have found. Instead of eating it myself I have kept it for you as a perquisite of your royal office. So take it.' The monkey went at it carelessly and was caught in the snare. When he accused the fox of laying a trap for him, the fox replied: 'Fancy a fool like you, friend monkey, being king of the animals!'

¶ People who attempt things without due consideration suffer for it and get laughed at into the bargain.

DEAD MEN TELL NO TALES

A fox and a monkey, as they journeyed together, disputed at great length about the nobility of their lineage. When they reached a certain place on the road, the monkey fixed his gaze upon it and uttered a groan. The fox asked what was wrong with him. The monkey pointed to some tombs that stood there. 'Don't you expect me to mourn,' he said, 'when I behold the sepulchres of the slaves and freedmen of my ancestors?' 'Lie away to your heart's content,' answered the fox. 'They won't any of them rise up to contradict you.'

¶ It is the same with men who are imposters. They never boast more loudly than when there is no one to expose them.

LOOK BEFORE YOU LEAP

A fox tumbled into a water tank and could not get out. Along came a thirsty goat, and seeing the fox asked him if the water was good. The fox jumped at the chance. He sang the praises of the water with all the eloquence at his command and urged the goat to come down. The goat was so thirsty that he went down without stopping to think and drank his fill. Then they began to consider how they were to get up again. 'I have a good idea,' said the fox, 'that is, if you are willing to do something to help us both. Be so kind as to place your forefeet against the wall and hold your horns straight up. Then I can nip up, and pull you up too.' The goat was glad enough to comply. The fox clambered nimbly over his haunches, shoulders, and horns, reached the edge of the tank, and began to make off. The goat complained that he had broken their compact. But he only came back to say: 'You have more hairs in your beard than brains in your head, my friend. Otherwise, you wouldn't have gone down without thinking how you were going to get up.'

¶ A sensible man never embarks on an enterprise until he can see his way clear to the end of it.

CUT OFF YOUR TAILS TO SAVE
MY FACE!

A fox who had lost his tail in a trap was so ashamed of the disfigurement that he felt life was not worth living. So he decided to persuade all the other foxes to maim themselves in the same way; then, he thought, his own loss would not be so conspicuous. He collected them all and advised them to cut off their tails. A tail, he said, was merely a superfluous appendage, ugly to look at and heavy to carry. But one of the others answered: 'Look here! You only give us this advice because it suits your own book.'

¶ This tale satirizes those who offer advice to their neighbours not out of benevolence but from self-interest.

THE FOX AND THE MASK

A fox entered an actor's house and rummaged through all his properties. Among other things he found a mask representing a hobgoblin's head – the work of a talented artist. He took it up in his paws and said: 'What a fine head! A pity it has no brain in it!'

¶ This fable reminds us that some men of impressive physical appearance are deficient in intellect.

A LESSON FOR FOOLS

A crow sat in a tree holding in his beak a piece of meat that he had stolen. A fox which saw him determined to get the meat. It stood under the tree and began to tell the crow what a beautiful big bird he was. He ought to be king of all the birds, the fox said; and he would undoubtedly have been made king, if only he had a voice as well. The crow was so anxious to prove that he *had* a voice, that he dropped the meat and croaked for all he was worth. Up ran the fox, snapped up the meat, and said to him: 'If you added brains to all your other qualifications, you would make an ideal king.'

ONE-WAY TRAFFIC

An old lion, who was too weak to hunt or fight for his food, decided that he must get it by his wits. He lay down in a cave, pretending to be ill, and whenever any animals came to visit him, he seized them and ate them. When many had perished in this way, a fox who had seen through the trick came and stood at a distance from the cave, and inquired how he was. 'Bad,' the lion answered, and asked why he did not come in. 'I would have come in,' said the fox, 'but I saw a lot of tracks going in and none coming out.'

¶ A wise man recognizes danger signals in time to avoid injury.

REAPING WITHOUT SOWING

A lion and a bear began fighting over a fawn which they had found, and mauled each other so badly that they lost consciousness and lay half-dead. A fox which passed by, seeing them incapable and the fawn lying between them, picked it up and threaded his way out from among them. Unable to get up, they said: 'A grievous fate is ours – to undergo all this suffering for the benefit of a fox.'

¶ People have good reason to be distressed when they see the fruits of their own labours borne away by chance comers.

TAUGHT BY EXPERIENCE

A lion, a donkey, and a fox formed a partnership and went out hunting. When they had taken a quantity of game the lion told the donkey to share it out. The donkey divided it into three equal parts and bade the lion choose one – on which the lion leapt at him in a fury and devoured him. Then he told the fox to divide it. The fox collected nearly all of it into one pile, leaving only a few trifles for himself, and told the lion to make his choice. The lion asked who taught him to share things in that way. 'What happened to the donkey,' he answered.

¶ We learn wisdom by seeing the misfortunes of others.

THE FOX OUT-FOXED

An ass and a fox made an alliance and went out hunting. When a lion appeared in their path, the fox realized the danger that threatened them, and going up to the lion he undertook to hand over the ass to him in exchange for a guarantee of security. On receiving the lion's promise to let him go, he led the ass into a trap. But the lion, when he saw that the ass could not possibly escape, seized the fox first and then went after the ass at his leisure.

¶ Those who plot against their friends often find to their surprise that they destroy themselves into the bargain.

BLOOD-SUCKERS

Aesop spoke in the public assembly at Samos when a demagogue was being tried for his life. 'A fox which was crossing a river,' he said, 'was carried into a deep gully, and all his efforts to get out were unavailing. Besides all the other suffering that he had to endure, he was tormented by a swarm of ticks which fastened on him. A hedgehog which came that way on its travels was sorry for him and asked if it should pick off the ticks. "No, please don't," replied the fox. "Why not?" said the hedgehog. "Because these have already made a good meal on me, and don't suck much blood now. But if you take them away, another lot will come, all hungry, and drain every drop of blood I have left."

'It is the same with you, men of Samos,' said Aesop. 'This man will do you no more harm, for he is rich. But if you kill him, others will come who are still hungry, and they will go on stealing until they have emptied your treasury.'

MEN AND LIONS

Once upon a time a lion and a man were travelling together, and both of them were talking boastfully. By the roadside stood a block of stone on which was carved the image of a man throttling a lion. The man pointed a sly finger at it and said to his companion: 'You see, we men are stronger than you.' A smile flickered on the lion's face. 'If lions knew how to carve,' said he, 'you would often see a man with a lion on top of him.'

¶ Many people who talk boastfully about their courage and hardihood are shown up by the gruelling test of experience.

IT IS QUALITY NOT QUANTITY
THAT COUNTS

A vixen sneered at a lioness because she never bore more than one cub. 'Only one,' she replied, 'but a lion.'

DISARMED

A lion fell in love with a farmer's daughter and wooed her. The farmer could not bear to give his girl in marriage to a wild beast; yet he dared not refuse. So he evaded the difficulty by telling the importunate suitor that, while he quite approved of him as a husband for his daughter, he could not give her to him unless he would pull out his teeth and cut off his claws, because the girl was afraid of them. The lion was so much in love that he readily submitted to these sacrifices. But when he presented himself again, the farmer treated him with contempt and cudgelled him off the premises.

¶ Do not be too ready to take advice which is offered you. If nature has given you special advantages over others, do not let yourself be deprived of them, or you will fall an easy prey to people who used to stand in awe of you.

THIRD-PARTY PROFIT

On a hot, thirsty summer's day a lion and a boar came to drink at a small spring. They started quarrelling which should drink first, and so provoked each other to a mortal combat. But stopping for a moment to take breath, they looked round and saw some vultures waiting to devour whichever of them was killed. This sight made them stop their quarrel. 'It is better for us to be friends,' they said, 'than to be eaten by vultures and crows.'

¶ Strife and contention are ill things, which end in danger for all parties, if they have not the sense to be reconciled.

A BIRD IN THE HAND

A lion was just going to devour a hare which he had found asleep, when he saw a deer go by. So he left the hare to pursue the deer, and the hare, awakened by the noise, ran away. After a long chase the lion found he could not catch the deer, and when he went back to get the hare he found that it too had taken to flight. 'It serves me right,' he said, 'for letting go the food I had in my grasp, in the hope of getting something better.'

¶ Men are sometimes like this lion. Instead of being content with a moderate gain, they are attracted by some more alluring prospect – and are surprised to find that they lose even what they could have been sure of having.

THE LION'S SHARE

A lion and a wild ass were hunting – the lion using his strength and the ass his swiftness of foot. When they had caught a number of animals the lion divided them into three lots. 'I will take the first lot,' he said, 'because as king I hold the highest rank; and the second one, as your equal partner. As for this third one, it will bring you into serious trouble unless you choose to make yourself scarce.'

¶ Whatever he undertakes, a man should estimate his capacity according to his own powers, and not enter into alliance or tie himself up with people who are too strong for him.

A COMPANION IN FEAR

The lion was continually finding fault with Prometheus. It was true that Prometheus had made him big and handsome, had armed his jaws with teeth and his paws with claws, and had given him greater strength than any other animal. But with all these advantages, he complained, he was afraid of cocks. 'You have no reason to blame me,' replied Prometheus. 'You have everything that *I* could give you, every gift it was in my power to fashion for you. It is your own spirit that has this one weakness.' At this the lion was sorrowful and kept accusing himself of cowardice, till at length he wanted to die. But while he was in this frame of mind he met an elephant, and after greeting him stopped for a talk. He noticed that the elephant kept moving his ears all the time. 'What's the matter?' he asked. 'Can't you keep your ears still for one moment?' It happened just then that a gnat flew round the elephant's head. 'Do you see that tiny buzzing thing?' he asked. 'If it gets into the passage of my ear, it's all over with me.' 'There's no need now for me to die,' said the lion. 'I am big and strong, and I'm more fortunate than the elephant. A cock is at any rate something more to be afraid of than a gnat.'

THE MIGHTY FALLEN

When a man loses the prestige that he once had, he becomes in his misfortune the plaything even of cowards.

A lion worn out with age and feebleness lay breathing his last. First came a boar and with a blow from its flashing tusks took revenge on him for an old injury. Then a bull lowered its horns and gored its enemy's body. An ass, seeing these attacks delivered with impunity, started kicking the lion's forehead with its heels. The lion was on the point of expiring. 'It was hard enough to bear,' he said, 'when those brave animals triumphed over me. But as for you, you shameful blot on creation, to be at your mercy as I die is like dying twice over.'

A RESPECTER OF PERSONS

A lion was standing over a bullock which he had felled, when a bandit presented himself and demanded a share of it. 'I would give it you,' said the lion, 'if you were not a habitual plunderer yourself.' With that, he drove the ruffian away. It happened that an inoffensive traveller came that way. On seeing the wild animal he stepped back. But the lion was as gentle as could be. 'There,' he said, 'you shall have a share for not being greedy. Do not be afraid to take it,' And after dividing the carcass he went off into the woods, to give the man a chance of getting at it.

¶ A very good example, deserving all praise. Yet it is avarice that grows rich while meekness remains poor.

NEGOTIATING FROM WEAKNESS

When the hares addressed a public meeting and claimed that all should have fair shares, the lions answered: 'A good speech, Hairy-Feet, but it lacks claws and teeth such as we have.'

A PLOTTER OUT-PLOTTED

An old lion lay sick in a cave, and all the animals came to visit their king except the fox. The wolf seized this chance to speak ill of the fox in the lion's hearing, saying he had no respect for their lord and master, and that was why he had not even visited him. The fox himself arrived in time to hear the last part of what the wolf was saying. The lion roared threaten-ingly at him, but the fox begged leave to make his defence. 'Which,' he asked, 'of the animals here assembled has rendered you as great a service as I have? I have travelled everywhere seeking from doc-tors a cure for your sickness, and I have found one.' The lion demanded to know then and there what the cure was. 'You must flay a wolf alive,' replied the fox, 'and put the hide on yourself while it is still warm.' In a moment the wolf lay dead. 'One should not provoke the master to ill feeling,' said the fox with a laugh, 'but encourage his better feelings.'

¶ The man who plots against another plots his own destruction.

THE WAGES OF TREACHERY

The wolves once said to the dogs: 'Since you are exactly like us, why do you not come to a brotherly understanding with us? There is no difference between us except in our ways of thinking. We live in freedom. You cringe like slaves to men, letting them beat you and put collars on you, and guarding their flocks for them; and when they eat they only throw the bones to you. Take our advice. Hand over all the flocks to us; then we will share them between us and gorge ourselves.' The dogs listened to this proposal. But as soon as the wolves got inside the fold they started by killing the dogs.

¶ Such is the reward of traitors to their own country.

ALWAYS IN THE WRONG

A wolf, seeing a lamb drinking from a river, wanted to find a specious pretext for devouring him. He stood higher up the stream and accused the lamb of muddying the water so that he could not drink. The lamb said that he drank only with the tip of his tongue, and that in any case he was standing lower down the river, and could not possibly disturb the water higher up. When this excuse failed him the wolf said: 'Well, last year you insulted my father.' 'I wasn't even born then,' replied the lamb. 'You are good at finding answers,' said the wolf, 'but I'm going to eat you all the same.'

¶ When a man is determined to get his knife into someone, he will turn a deaf ear to any plea, however just.

KINDNESS ILL REQUITED

A wolf which had swallowed a bone went about looking for someone to relieve him of it. Meeting a heron, he offered it a fee to remove the bone. The heron put its head down his throat, pulled out the bone and then claimed the promised reward. 'Are you not content, my friend,' said the wolf, 'to have got your head safe and sound out of a wolf's mouth, but you must demand a fee as well?'

¶ When one does a bad man a service, the only recompense one can hope for is that he will not add injury to ingratitude.

THE POT CALLS THE KETTLE
BLACK

A wolf was carrying to his lair a sheep which he had lifted from a flock, when a lion met him and took it from him. The wolf stood at a safe distance and cried: 'You have no right to take away my property.' 'You came by it rightfully of course,' replied the lion with a laugh. 'No doubt it was a present from a friend.'

¶ This story is a satire on thieves and greedy robbers who fall foul of one another when they are out of luck.

A COMMUNIST DICTATOR

A wolf which had been made leader of the other wolves established a law that each of them should put into a pool everything he caught in the chase and share it equally with all the rest, so that they should not be driven by hunger to eat one another. But an ass came forward and, shaking his mane, said: 'Out of the mind of the wolf has come forth a noble thought. But how is it, wolf, that you yourself laid up in your den the quarry you took yesterday? Put it in the common store and share it.' This exposure shamed the wolf into annulling his laws.

¶ The very men who pretend to legislate justly do not themselves abide by the laws which they enact and administer.

MISPLACED CONFIDENCE

A wolf began to follow a flock of sheep, but did them no harm. At first the shepherd feared it as an enemy and kept his eye on it carefully. But when it continued to accompany them without making the slightest attempt at robbery, he thought it was more like a protector than a designing foe, and having occasion to go to the city he left the flock with it in attendance. The wolf saw its chance, and falling on the sheep tore most of them to pieces. When the shepherd returned and saw his flock destroyed, he said: 'I have got what I deserved for entrusting sheep to a wolf.'

¶ It is the same with men. Those who deposit valuables in the hands of money-grubbers must expect to lose them.

BORN PLUNDERERS

A shepherd who found some wolf cubs reared them with great care, hoping that when they grew up they would not only guard his own sheep but would seize others and bring them to him. But as soon as they had grown big and found a safe opportunity, they began by worrying their master's flock. 'It serves me right,' he said with a groan when he saw what they had done. 'Even if these animals had been full-grown I should have had to find some way of destroying them. So what sense was there in sparing them when they were babies?'

¶ If you save a bad man's life, you – though you may not realize it – will be the first victim of the power which you thus enable him to obtain.

TRYING TO MAKE A SILK PURSE
OUT OF A SOW'S EAR

A shepherd took a new-born wolf cub which he had found and brought him up with his dogs till he was full grown. Whenever a sheep was stolen by another wolf, this one joined with the dogs in pursuit. And if the dogs had to return without catching the marauder, he went on till he overtook him, and then – like the wolf he was – shared the plunder with him. Sometimes, too, when there had been no robbery, he secretly killed a sheep himself and shared it with the dogs, until in the end the shepherd guessed what was going on and hanged him on a tree.

¶ A vicious nature will never make a good man.

DELUSION

Wandering in a lonely place as the sun went down, a wolf noticed the long shadow cast by his body. 'Fancy a big fellow like me being afraid of a lion!' he said. 'Why, I must be thirty yards long! I'll make myself king and rule all the animals, every single one of them.' But for all his boasting, a strong lion caught him and sat down to devour him. Too late, he regretted his mistake. 'Conceit,' he wailed, 'has helped to bring about my ruin.'

A CASE OF MISTAKEN IDENTITY

A wolf thought that by disguising himself he could get plenty to eat. Putting on a sheepskin to trick the shepherd, he joined the flock at grass without being discovered. At nightfall the shepherd shut him with the sheep in the fold and made it fast all round by blocking the entrance. Then, feeling hungry, he picked up his knife and slaughtered an animal for his supper. It happened to be the wolf.

¶ Assuming a character that does not belong to one can involve one in serious trouble. Such play-acting has cost many a man his life.

SECOND THOUGHTS

Once upon a time the hares held a meeting and bewailed the insecurity and fear in which they lived – the prey of men, dogs, eagles, and many other animals. It was better, they said, to die and have done with it than to live all their lives in terror and trembling. Thus resolved, they ran all together to a pool with the intention of jumping in and drowning themselves. Some frogs which were squatting round the pool, the moment they heard the patter of running feet, scuttled into the water. At this, one of the hares, who evidently had his wits about him more than the rest, said: 'Stop, all of you, don't do anything rash. For you see now that there are creatures even more tormented by fear than we are.'

¶ It is comforting to the wretched to see others in worse case than they are themselves.

READY FOR ACTION

A wild boar was standing against a tree and whetting his tusks. A fox asked why he sharpened them when no huntsman was pursuing him and no danger threatened. 'I have a reason for doing so,' he replied. 'If danger overtakes me, I shall not have time then to sharpen them, but they will be all ready for use.'

¶ Do not wait till danger is at hand to make your preparations.

A mouse ran over the body of a sleeping lion. Waking up, the lion seized it and was minded to eat it. But when the mouse begged to be released, promising to repay him if he would spare it, he laughed and let it go. Not long afterwards its gratitude was the means of saving his life. Being captured by hunters, he was tied by a rope to a tree. The mouse heard his groans, and running to the spot freed him by gnawing through the rope. 'You laughed at me the other day,' it said, 'because you did not expect me to repay your kindness. Now you see that even mice are grateful.'

¶ A change of fortune can make the strongest man need a weaker man's help.

PRIDE WILL HAVE A FALL

The mice, who were at war with the weasels, were always getting the worst of it. They held a meeting, and, coming to the conclusion that their defeats were due to the lack of leadership, they chose some of their number and elected them generals. These, in order to distinguish themselves from the rest, made horns and fixed them on their heads. When they joined battle their whole army was routed and took to flight. They all got safely into their holes except the generals, who, unable to get in on account of their horns, were caught and devoured.

¶ Vainglory is often the cause of misfortune.

TOWN MOUSE AND COUNTRY MOUSE

A field-mouse invited a friend who lived in a town house to dine with him in the country. The other accepted with alacrity; but when he found that the fare consisted only of barley and other corn, he said to his host: 'Let me tell you, my friend, you live like an ant. But I have abundance of good things to eat, and if you will come home with me you shall share them all.' So the two of them went off at once; and when his friend showed him peas and beans, bread, dates, cheese, honey, and fruit, the astonished field-mouse congratulated him heartily and cursed his own lot. They were about to begin their meal when the door suddenly opened, and the timid creatures were so scared by the sound that they scuttled into chinks. When they had returned and were just going to take some dried figs, they saw someone else come into the room to fetch something, and once more they jumped to take cover in their holes. At this the field-mouse decided that he did not care if he had to go hungry. 'Good-bye, my friend,' he said with a groan. 'You may eat your fill and enjoy yourself. But your good cheer costs you dear in danger and fear. I would rather gnaw my poor meals of barley and corn without being afraid or having to watch anyone out of the corner of my eye.'

❡ A simple life with peace and quiet is better than faring luxuriously and being tortured by fear.

WE GET THE RULERS WE DESERVE

The frogs were tired of having no one to govern them, and sent a deputation to Zeus to ask for a king. He saw how simple they were. So first of all he just dropped a block of wood in the pond. For a moment they were frightened by the splash and dived to the bottom. Then, since the wood stayed quite still, they came to the surface, and in the end they became so contemptuous of it that they jumped up and squatted on it. Thinking it undignified to be ruled by such a thing, they approached Zeus again and asked him to change their king; this one, they said, was too easy-going. Losing patience with them, he sent them a water-snake, which devoured as many of them as it could catch.

¶ This fable teaches us that we are better off with an indolent and harmless ruler than with a mischief-making tyrant.

ONE IS ENOUGH

All the animals were making merry one summer's day over the Sun's wedding, and among the rest the frogs were rejoicing. But one of their number said: 'You fools, why all this jubilation? One sun is enough to dry up all the muddy pools. If he marries a wife and begets a child like himself, we shall be in a bad way.'

¶ A lot of empty-headed people rejoice over the wrong things.

A VOICE AND NOTHING MORE

A lion's attention was attracted by the croak of a frog, which he thought from the sound must be some big animal. After waiting for a short while he saw the frog come out of its pool. Running up and crushing it with his foot he cried: 'Fancy such a little thing as you making such a big noise!'

¶ This fable satirizes people with itching tongues, who can do nothing but talk.

MAKING THE PUNISHMENT FIT
THE CRIME

A land rat, in an evil hour, struck up a friendship with a frog, who played a mean trick on him. He tied the rat's foot to his own. They started out on dry land to get themselves a dinner. But when they came to the edge of a pond, the frog dived in. *He* revelled in the water and kept on uttering his familiar croak, while the unlucky rat, who was dragged down with him, swallowed a bellyful and was drowned. But his dead body floated, still made fast to the frog's foot. A kite that spotted it snatched it up in its claws, and the frog, unable to free himself, was hoisted up with it. So the kite ate him too.

¶ Even when you are dead you can get even with an enemy. For nothing escapes the eye of divine Justice; it weighs crimes in the balance and allots the appropriate punishment.

TOO BIG FOR HER SKIN

For the weak to try to imitate the strong is courting destruction.

Once upon a time a frog saw an ox in a meadow and was envious of its huge bulk. So she swelled out her body till all the wrinkles disappeared and then asked her children if she was now fatter than the ox. 'No,' they said. With a still greater effort she stretched her skin tight, and asked which was the bigger now. 'The ox,' they answered. At last she got cross, and making frantic efforts to blow herself out still more, she burst herself and died.

A LESSON LEARNT TOO LATE

A bird in a cage at a window used to sing at night-time. A bat which heard her came up and asked why she never sang by day, but only at night. She explained that there was a good reason: it was while she was singing once in the daytime that she was captured, and this had taught her a lesson. 'It's no good taking precautions now,' said the bat. 'You should have been careful before you were caught.'

¶ The moral is that it is too late to be sorry after you have let things go wrong.

DOUBLY DISABLED

A mole declared to his mother that he could see – a thing moles cannot do. To try him, his mother gave him a lump of frankincense and asked him what it was. 'A pebble,' he replied. 'My child,' she said, 'you not only cannot see: you have lost your sense of smell as well.'

¶ When people profess to do what is impossible, the simplest test will often show them up for the impostors they are.

THE IMITATIVE INSTINCT

A monkey sitting in a lofty tree saw some fishermen casting their net into a river and watched what they did. When they left the net and went some distance away to eat their meal, he came down from his tree and tried to copy them – as they say monkeys always will. But as soon as he touched the net he got entangled in it and was in danger of drowning. 'Mine is a just punishment,' he thought, 'for trying to fish when I hadn't learnt how to.'

¶ If you meddle with what does not concern you, far from gaining anything, you will have reason to regret it.

A CLUMSY LIAR

Travellers by sea often take with them Maltese lap-dogs or monkeys, to while away the time during their voyage. One such traveller had a monkey. When they were off Cape Sunium on the coast of Attica a violent storm arose, in which the ship capsized and everyone on board, including the monkey, had to jump over-board and swim. A dolphin which saw the monkey mistook him for a man, and taking him on its back it carried him to land. On reaching Piraeus, the port of the Athenians, it asked the monkey if he was Athenian born. When the monkey said he was, adding that his parents were illustrious citizens of Athens, the dol-phin asked if he knew Piraeus too. The monkey took Piraeus to be a man; so he said he knew him very well – in fact he was one of his best friends. This whopping lie so enraged the dolphin that it tipped him into the water and left him to drown.

¶ This fable satirizes people who, ignorant of the truth, think they can make others swallow a pack of lies.

KILLED BY KINDNESS

It is said that apes produce twins, on one of which they lavish affection, feeding it with great care, while they turn against the other and neglect it. But by a curious dispensation of providence, the one that the mother delights to care for and strains tightly to her breast is smothered to death, while the rejected one reaches maturity.

¶ No forethought can prevail against destiny.

A BLOOD FEUD

A snake crawled up to a countryman's child and killed it. Provoked by this outrage, the father took an axe and waited at the snake's hole, ready to strike it as soon as it came out. When it put its head out he brought down the axe, but missed it and chipped the rock instead. After that he was on his guard against reprisals, and asked his enemy to be reconciled with him. But the snake refused. 'No,' it said, 'I cannot be on good terms with you when I see that cut in the rock, nor you with me when you look at your son's grave.'

¶ A serious quarrel cannot be lightly made up.

53
EVIL FOR GOOD

One winter's day a farm-hand found a snake frozen
stiff with the cold, and moved by compassion he
picked it up and put it in his bosom. But with the
warmth its natural instinct returned, and it gave its
benefactor a fatal bite. As he died he said: 'I have got
what I deserve for taking pity on an evil creature.'

¶ This story shows that even the greatest kindness
cannot change a bad nature.

CURSED ABOVE ALL CATTLE

Timeo Danaos et dona ferentes

When Zeus was celebrating his wedding feast all the animals brought him such presents as they were able to bring. The serpent crawled up to heaven with a rose in its mouth. But at the sight of it Zeus said: 'I will accept gifts from all other creatures, but from your mouth I will have nothing.'

¶ Favours are frightening when they come from evildoers.

UNITED AGAINST THE
COMMON FOE

A snake and a weasel started fighting together in the house where they lived, instead of killing the mice as both of them were in the habit of doing. When the mice saw them at it they came walking out of their holes. The sight of the mice put an end to the battle; for the combatants at once turned to attack their old enemies.

¶ The same thing is seen in politics. When people mix themselves up in the quarrels of rival demagogues, they find, too late, that both parties unite to destroy them.

THE BEST METHOD OF DEFENCE

A snake was trodden on by so many people that it went and complained to Zeus. 'If you had bitten the first man who trod on you,' said Zeus, 'the next one would have thought twice about doing it.'

¶ Those who stand up to a first assailant make others afraid of them.

VENGEANCE AT ANY PRICE

A wasp settled on a snake's head and tormented it by continually stinging. The snake, maddened with the pain and not knowing how else to be revenged on its tormentor, put its head under the wheel of a waggon, so that they both perished together.

¶ Some men elect to die with their enemies rather than let them live.

A BITER BIT

Any rascal who tries to get his teeth into someone with a sharper bite than his own may recognize his likeness in the following fable.

A snake entered a smith's workshop. Looking round for something to eat, it bit a file. 'What's the good of trying to mark me with your teeth, you fool?' said the file defiantly. 'I have a way of gnawing through every piece of iron I meet.'

ILL-JUDGED RIVALRY

At an assembly of the beasts a monkey stood up and danced. The whole company thought highly of its performance and applauded with such enthusiasm that a camel was jealous and desired to earn similar praise. So up it got and tried to dance like the monkey. But it made such a ridiculous exhibition of itself that the angry spectators cudgelled it out of their sight.

¶ This tale shows what happens to people who are tempted by envy to compete with their betters.

CAUGHT ON THE BLIND SIDE

A deer which was blind in one eye went to graze on the sea/shore, turning its good eye landwards, on the watch for the approach of hunters, and the injured eye to the sea, from which it did not expect any danger. But some men who came coasting inshore saw it and shot it down. As it was dying it thought: 'Unlucky that I am! I was on my guard against the attack which I knew might come from the land, but the sea, from which I thought no danger threatened, has proved yet more deadly.'

¶ Our expectations are often deceived. Things which we feared might do us hurt turn out to our advantage, and what we thought would save us proves our ruin.

BITTEN BUT NOT SHY

A lion which had fallen sick was lying in a cave. He said to his beloved comrade the fox: 'If you want me to recover and live, use your honeyed tongue to entice the big deer which lives in the forest to come within reach of my claws. I am hungry for his guts and his heart.' The fox went off and found the deer frisking in the woods. Joining in its play he greeted it with these words: 'I have come to bring you good news. You know that our king the lion is my neighbour. Well, he is ill and near to death, and he has been considering which of the animals is to reign after him. The pig, he says, is a senseless brute, the bear is a lazy-bones, the leopard bad-tempered, and the tiger a braggart; the deer is the best qualified for the throne, because his height is impressive, because he is a long-lived animal, and because his horns frighten the snakes. So, to cut a long story short, you have been nominated as king. What are you going to give me for being the first to bring you the news? Tell me quickly, for I am in a hurry; the lion relies on my counsel in everything he does, and he may be wanting me back. If you will listen to an old fox's advice, I think you should come with me and stay with him till he dies.'

At this speech the deer's mind was puffed up with conceit, and it went to the cave without any suspicion of what was going to happen. The lion pounced upon it eagerly; but he only succeeded in tearing its ears with his claws, and the deer hastened to escape in the woods. The fox beat his paws together in disappoint‚ ment at having wasted his pains, and the lion moaned and roared aloud in his hunger and mortification. Eventually he begged the fox to have another try and lure the deer back again. 'It is a difficult and trouble‚ some task that you are laying on me,' the fox replied, 'but all the same I will do it for you.' And weaving his cunning toils he started tracking the deer like a hunting dog, and asked some shepherds if they had seen a deer with blood about it. They pointed out the wood into which it had gone; and finding it there cooling itself after its hurried flight, he accosted it as bold as brass. The deer's hair bristled with anger. 'You scoundrel,' it said, 'you won't catch me again. If you so much as come near me, you shall pay for it with your life. Go and fox other people, who don't know you. Find someone else to make a king of and drive mad.' 'Are you such a miserable coward,' the fox answered, 'and so suspicious of us who are your friends? When the lion caught hold of your ear he meant to give you his last advice and instructions, before he died, about your great responsibilities as king; but you could not bear even a scratch from the paw of a sick creature. And now he is even angrier than you are, and wants to make the wolf king. A bad master for us he would be. But come with me and don't be afraid; be as meek as any sheep. I swear by all the leaves and all the springs that the lion will not hurt you, and I will have no other master but you.' By this deceit he induced the unlucky deer to go with him again, and as soon as it entered the cave the lion made a meal of it, swallowing bones, marrow, and entrails. The fox stood looking on; and when the heart fell out of the carcass he stealthily snatched it and ate it as a reward for his trouble. The lion missed it and rummaged for it through all the fragments. 'You may as well stop searching,' said the fox from a safe distance, 'for the truth is, it hadn't a heart. What sort of heart do you expect to find in a creature which twice came into a lion's den and within reach of his paws?'

¶ Men's lust for glory clouds their minds so that they do not perceive the dangers that beset them.

A BREED OF FAINT-HEARTS

A fawn once said to the old deer: 'Father, nature has made you bigger and swifter than dogs, and moreover you have marvellous horns to defend yourself with. Why then do you flee from them in such terror?' 'What you say is quite true, my son,' replied the deer with a laugh. 'I don't know how it is; but I do know that the moment I hear the baying of a hound I feel an irresistible impulse to run away.'

¶ If a man is born a coward, no amount of exhortation can put a stout heart into him.

THE IRONY OF FATE

A thirsty stag came to a spring, and after drinking noticed his own reflection in the water. He felt proud of his great and curiously fashioned antlers, but was very dissatisfied with his slender weak-looking legs. While he was still lost in thought a lion appeared and ran to him. He fled and easily outdistanced it – for the deer's strength is in his legs, the lion's in his courageous heart. As long as the ground was open, the stag kept safely in front; but when they reached wooded country his antlers got entangled in the branches of a tree, so that he could not run farther and was caught by the lion. As he was about to be killed, 'Alas!' he thought, 'my legs, which I feared would fail me, were my preservation, and the antlers that filled me with such confidence are destroying me.'

¶ It often happens, when we are in danger, that the friends whose loyalty we doubted prove our saviours, while those in whom we put implicit trust betray us.

HOW THE TORTOISE GOT
ITS SHELL

Zeus was entertaining all the animals at his wedding feast. Only the tortoise stayed away, and Zeus could not think why. So next day he asked it why it did not come with the others. 'There's no place like home,' it replied – an answer which angered Zeus so much that he made it carry its own house about on its back.

¶ Many men would rather have plain fare at home than live on the fat of the land in other people's houses.

A WASTE OF GOOD COUNSEL

A tortoise asked an eagle to teach it to fly. The eagle pointed out that it was ill-adapted by nature for flight, but the tortoise only importuned him the more. So the eagle, taking it up in his talons, bore it to a great height and let it go. It fell at the foot of some rocks and was dashed to pieces.

¶ A spirit of rivalry will often make men disregard the advice of wiser heads with fatal results for themselves.

SLOW BUT SURE

A tortoise and a hare started to dispute which of them was the swifter, and before separating they made an appointment for a certain time and place to settle the matter. The hare had such confidence in its natural fleetness that it did not trouble about the race but lay down by the wayside and went to sleep. The tortoise acutely conscious of its slow movements, padded along without ever stopping until it passed the sleeping hare and won the race.

¶ A naturally gifted man, through lack of application, is often beaten by a plodder.

THE REWARD OF THE WICKED

An eagle and a vixen became friends and decided to live near each other in the hope that closer acquaintance would cement their friendship. The eagle flew to the top of a very tall tree and laid her eggs there, while the vixen gave birth to her cubs in a thicket underneath. One day she went off in search of food. The eagle, feeling hungry, swooped into the bushes, snatched up the cubs, and made a meal of them with her brood. The vixen came back and saw what had happened. She was less distressed by the loss of her young than by the difficulty of punishing the eagle. How could she, tied down to earth as she was, pursue a bird? All she could do was to stand far off and curse her enemy – like any weak and feeble creature. But it chanced before long that the eagle was punished for violating the sanctity of friendship. Some men were sacrificing a goat in a field, and the eagle darted down onto the altar and carried off a burning piece of offal to her nest. Just then a strong wind sprang up and fanned into a blaze the bits of dry stalk of which the nest was made. The result was that the nestlings, which were not yet fully fledged, were burnt and fell to the ground. The vixen ran to the spot and gobbled up every one of them right under the eagle's eyes.

¶ The point of this tale is that those who break a compact of friendship, even though the friend they have wronged may be powerless to punish them, cannot escape the vengeance of heaven.

REPAYMENT IN KIND

A farm labourer who found an eagle caught in a
snare was so struck by its beauty that he let it go free.
The eagle showed him that it was not ungrateful for
this deliverance. Seeing him sitting one day under a
crumbling wall, it flew up and snatched in its talons
the headband that he was wearing. The man jumped
up and pursued it; the eagle then dropped the band,
and he picked it up. On returning he found how
wonderfully the bird had repaid his kindness. The
wall had collapsed just where he had been sitting.

THE JACKDAW WHO WOULD
BE AN EAGLE

An eagle flew down from a high rock and seized a lamb. The sight made a jackdaw envious, and in his eagerness to emulate the eagle he swooped down with a great whir of his wings onto the back of a ram. But his claws got entangled in the fleece, and he beat his wings in a vain attempt to free himself, until the shepherd, seeing what had occurred, ran up and took him. He clipped the wings that used to bear the bird so swiftly, and at nightfall carried him home for his children. When they asked what kind of bird it was, '*I* know he's a jackdaw,' he said, 'but *he* tries to pass for an eagle.'

¶ If you try to rival someone stronger than yourself, not only do you waste your pains, but your misfortunes are laughed at into the bargain.

HOPE DEFERRED

A hungry jackdaw had perched on a fig tree, and finding that the figs were still hard was waiting for them to ripen. A fox who noticed that it had become a fixture there inquired the reason, and, on being told, said: 'It is a mistake to let hope engross your attention. Hope can only delude you; it will never fill your belly.'

GETTING THE WORST OF
BOTH WORLDS

A jackdaw looked down on its fellows because it happened to be bigger than any of them. So it joined the crows and asked to be allowed to live with them. But as its appearance and voice were unfamiliar the crows knocked it about and chivied it off. Whereupon it returned to the daws. Indignant, however, at the way it had insulted them, they would not have it back. Thus it found itself banished from the society of both.

¶ The same thing happens to men who leave their native land because they prefer to live elsewhere. As foreigners, they are without honour in their new home, and they are disliked by their own countrymen for having treated them with such contempt.

BORROWED PLUMES

Intending to set up a king over the birds, Zeus appointed a day for them all to appear before him, when he would choose the most handsome to reign over them. They all went to a river bank and proceeded to do their toilet. A jackdaw, realizing how plain he was, went about collecting the feathers which the others moulted, and fastened them all over his body so that he was the gayest of them all. On the appointed day they all paraded in front of Zeus, including the daw in his motley plumage. Zeus was just going to award the throne to him because of his striking appearance, when the others indignantly plucked off his finery, each one taking the feathers that belonged to it. So he was stripped bare and changed back into a jackdaw.

¶ Men in debt are like this bird. They cut a dash on other people's money. Make them pay up, and you can recognize them for the nobodies they always were.

A BIRD IN THE HAND

A nightingale was perched on a tall oak tree, singing as they always do. A hawk saw her, and as he had nothing to eat, swooped down and snatched her up. She tried to escape from the jaws of death by begging him to let her go. She was too small, she said, to make a meal for a hawk; if he was hungry, he had better chase some bigger bird. But the hawk's answer was: 'I should be crazy if I let slip the food I have in my claws to go after something which is not yet in sight.'

¶ It is the same with human beings. It is senseless to let the hope of a bigger prize tempt you to give up what you have within your grasp.

BREACH OF PROMISE

A crow caught in a snare vowed to offer incense to Apollo if he would save him. But when his prayer was granted he forgot his promise. Afterwards he was caught again, and this time he gave Apollo the go-by and promised a sacrifice to Hermes. But Hermes said to him: 'Wretch, do you expect me to trust you when you have denied and defrauded your former patron?'

¶ Those who have shown ingratitude to bene-factors will not find others to help them when they are in a fix.

RIGHT OF ASYLUM

When the mistletoe first came into existence, the martin realized the danger that threatened the birds, and assembling them all together she advised them to tear it off, if possible, from the oaks on which it grew; if they could not manage this, they had best throw themselves on man's mercy and beg him not to use mistletoe glue to trap them. Since the other birds ridiculed the martin as a vain babbler, she went as a suppliant to mankind. They welcomed her for her prudence and took her to live with them. So, while other birds are caught and eaten by men, the martin is regarded as having taken sanctuary with them and nests without fear even in their houses.

¶ Those who foresee a danger naturally have a chance of avoiding it.

FIRESIDE SKETCH

A man bought a parrot, to which he gave the run of the house. It was quite tame, and jumping one day onto the hearth it perched there and kept up a pleasant chatter. The house cat eyed it, and asked who it was and where it came from. It said that the master had just bought it. 'Then most audacious of creatures,' said the cat, 'fancy a newcomer like you making such a noise, when I, who was born in the house, am not allowed to miaow! If ever I do, they are cross and chivy me away.' 'O mistress of the house,' answered the parrot, 'my advice to you is to take a long walk. You see, there's a difference. The family does not dislike my voice as it does yours.'

¶ This fable satirizes ill-natured critics who are always trying to find fault with others.

TIT FOR TAT

Do not do an ill turn to anyone. But if someone injures you, he deserves, according to the fable which I am going to relate, to be paid back in his own coin.

The story is that a stork which had arrived from foreign parts received an invitation to dinner from a fox, who served her with clear soup on a smooth slab of marble, so that the hungry bird could not taste a drop of it. Returning the invitation, the stork produced a flagon filled with pap, into which she stuck her bill and had a good meal, while her guest was tormented with hunger. 'You set the example,' she said, 'and you must not complain at my following it.'

NATURE'S PUNISHMENT OF
DISCONTENT

Kites originally had singing voices as clear as any swan. But when they heard horses neighing they were envious and did their best to imitate them. In trying to acquire this new trick, they lost the ability they already had: they could not learn to neigh and they forgot how to sing.

WHEN A MAN MEANS BUSINESS

A lark once made his nest in the green corn and fed his young on the tender shoots till they had crests on their heads and were fully fledged. One day when the owner inspected his land he saw that the crop was ripe and dry. 'It's time now,' he said, 'to call together all my friends to help me with the reaping.' One of the lark's crested chicks heard him and told its father, bidding him find another home to which they could move. 'There's no need to think of going yet awhile,' replied the father; 'the man who trusts friends to do a thing is in no great hurry about it.' When the farmer came again and saw the ears of corn dropping off in the heat of the sun, he said that he would hire reapers and sheaf-carriers the next day. 'Now it's really time for us to go somewhere else,' said the lark to his babies, 'when he relies on himself instead of his friends.'

SWAN SONG

A man who had heard that swans had very beautiful voices bought one which he happened to see exposed for sale. One day when he was giving a dinner party he went out and asked the swan to sing to his guests as they sat over their wine. But not a note could he get out of it. Some time afterwards, however, when it felt that it was going to die, it began to sing a dirge over its approaching end; for it is said that swans sing when they are at the point of death. When its owner heard it he said: 'If you sing only when you are dying, I was a fool to ask you for a song the other day. I'd have done better to prepare you for sacrifice.'

¶When people will not do a thing as a favour, they are sometimes made to do it against their will.

THE VICTOR VANQUISHED

A cock which had got the worst of a fight with its rival for the favours of the hens went and hid in a dark corner, while the victor climbed onto a high wall and crowed at the top of its voice. Immediately an eagle swooped down and snatched it up. The other was safe in its dark hiding-place, and was now able to woo the hens without fear of interruption.

¶ This story shows that God resists the proud but gives grace to the humble.

DISCRETION IS THE BETTER PART
OF VALOUR

A dog and a cock struck up a friendship and set out together on a journey. At nightfall the cock went up into a tree to sleep, while the dog made his bed in a hollow at its foot. The cock greeted the coming of dawn with his customary crow, and a vixen which heard it ran up and stood under the tree, bidding him come down to her; she would very much like, she said, to embrace the possessor of such a fine voice. The cock told her that she must first wake the porter who was sleeping down below, and ask for the door to be opened. 'Then I will come down,' he said. While she was looking for the porter to whom she was told to apply, the dog suddenly made one leap and tore her in pieces.

¶ Wise men, when attacked by an enemy, frus⟋ ⟍rate his design by sending him to someone better able to defend them than they are themselves.

A DIFFERENT POINT OF VIEW

Some thieves, on breaking into a house, found nothing in it but a cock, which they picked up and took away. They were about to sacrifice it, when it begged to be spared on the plea that it rendered men a useful service by waking them before daybreak to start their work. 'All the more reason for killing you,' was the reply; 'for by waking *them* you stop *us* from stealing.'

¶ What benefits honest men is the rogue's worst handicap.

MISPLACED CONFIDENCE

The halcyon is a bird that loves solitude and spends all its life over the sea, nesting in rocks on the coast, so they say, where men cannot pursue it. Once upon a time a halcyon which was about to breed came to a headland and built her nest on a rock overhanging the water. But one day when she had gone to find food the sea was whipped up by a squall, and a high wave washed over the nest and drowned the nestlings. 'Woe is me!' cried the bird when she returned and saw what had happened. 'I was on my guard against the traps that might be set for me on dry land, but this sea, to which I fled for refuge, has proved still more treacherous.'

¶ Some men act in a similar way. In their anxiety to protect themselves against their enemies they fail to realize that they are running into the arms of even more dangerous friends.

THE LAW OF SELF-PRESERVATION

A fowler spread his nets and tied his tame pigeons to them. Then he retired to a distance and waited for something to happen. In due course some wild pigeons came up and got entangled in the mesh. When the man hurried to the spot and began to lay hands on them, they reproached the tame birds for not giving warning when they saw their kindred walking into a trap. 'In our position,' the others replied, 'it is more important to avoid giving offence to our masters than to earn the gratitude of our kindred.'

¶ In the same way, slaves are not to be blamed if, in their anxiety to earn their masters' goodwill, they fail in affection towards their own relatives.

LOOK BEFORE YOU LEAP

A thirsty dove saw a jug of water in a picture. Mistaking it for a real one, it flew at it with a loud whir of its wings. The result was that it dashed itself against the picture, and falling on the ground with its wings injured was caught by a passer-by.

⁋ Do not go for things bald-headed. Men's passions sometimes tempt them to rush blindly into destruction.

87

BORN TO TROUBLE

A pigeon kept in a pigeonry boasted proudly of the large families that she reared. A crow, hearing her, said: 'That's enough bragging about that, my friend. The more children you have, the more wretched captives will there be to wring your heart.'

¶ The same applies to men who are slaves: the most miserable of all are those who beget children in servitude.

TRAITOR'S DEATH

A guest arrived rather late at the house of a bird-catcher. Not having anything else to offer him, the host went to fetch his tame partridge, intending to kill it. The partridge reproached him with ingratitude for thinking of destroying it, when it did him such good service by decoying its fellows into the nets and enabling him to catch them. 'All the more reason,' he said, 'for killing you, since you have no mercy even on your own kindred.'

¶ Treacherous friends are hateful not only to their victims but even to those to whom they betray them.

CHERISHING A VIPER

A hen found some serpent's eggs, which she hatched by carefully sitting on them and keeping them warm. A swallow which had watched her said: 'You fool, why do you rear creatures that, once they grow up, will make you the first victim of their evil-doing?'

¶ Even the kindest treatment cannot tame a savage nature.

THE PUNISHMENT OF SELFISHNESS

A horse and an ass were on a journey with their master. 'Take a share of my load,' said the ass to the horse, 'if you want to save my life.' But the horse would not, and the ass, worn out with fatigue, fell down and died. The master then put the whole load on the horse's back, and the ass's hide into the bargain. The horse began to groan and set up a piteous lament. 'Alas,' he cried, 'what misery have I let myself in for! I would not take a light load, and now look at me: I have to carry everything, hide and all.'

¶ The moral is that the strong should help the weak; so shall the lives of both be preserved.

SAVE US IN THE TIME OF TROUBLE

A soldier had a horse which, as long as he was at the wars, shared all his dangers and adventures and was well fed on barley. But when the war was over it was made to work like a slave, carrying heavy loads and getting nothing but chaff. War was declared again; and when the trumpets sounded the master bridled his horse, armed himself, and mounted. But the horse had no strength and stumbled at every step. 'You had better go and join an infantry regiment,' it said to him; 'for I am not worth calling a horse now. You have turned me into a donkey, and how can you expect to change me back again?'

¶ When you relax in times of security, it does not do to forget the day of affliction.

A BAD BARGAIN

A wild boar and a horse were grazing together. The boar was always spoiling the grass and muddying the water, and the horse, which wanted to pay him out for this, sought the aid of a huntsman. The man said that he could not do anything to help unless it would allow him to put a bridle on it and ride on its back. The horse was willing to consent to anything. So the man mounted on its back, and after overcoming the boar he took the horse home with him and tied it to the manger.

¶ Blind anger makes many people, in their eagerness to be revenged on their enemies, put themselves into someone else's power.

FELINE SOPHISTRY

A cat wanted to find a plausible excuse for killing and eating a cock which she had caught. She alleged that he made himself a nuisance to men by crowing at night and preventing them from sleeping. The cock's defence was that he did men a good turn by waking them to start their day's work. Then the cat charged him with committing the unnatural sin of incest with his mother and sisters. The cock replied that this also was a useful service to his owners, because it made the hens lay well. 'You are full of specious pleas,' said the cat; 'but that is no reason why I should go hungry. So she made a meal of him – showing how an evil nature is bent on wrongdoing, with or without the cloak of a fair-sounding pretext.

A house was overrun with mice. A cat which discovered this went there and caught and ate them one by one. These continual losses scared the survivors into their holes, where the cat could no longer get at them. So he decided that he must entice them out somehow. He climbed up the wall, hung himself on a peg, and shammed dead. But one of the mice, peeping out and seeing him, said: 'It's no use, my friend; I'll keep out of your way, even if you do turn yourself into a sack.'

¶ This fable can be applied to wise men. They learn by experience and are never deceived by the false pretences of an enemy.

VILLAINY UNMASKED

A cat heard that there were some sick hens on a farm. So he disguised himself as a doctor and presented himself there, complete with a bag of professional instruments. Outside the farmhouse he stood and called to the hens to ask how they were. 'Fine,' came the reply – 'if you will get off the premises.'

¶ A villain, try as he may to act the honest man, cannot fool a man of sense.

METAMORPHOSIS

Naturam expells furca, tamen usque recurret

A cat was enamoured of a handsome youth and begged Aphrodite to change her into a woman. The goddess, pitying her sad state, transformed her into a beautiful girl, and when the young man saw her he fell in love with her and took her home to be his wife. While they were resting in their bedroom, Aphrodite, who was curious to know if the cat's instincts had changed along with her shape, let a mouse loose in front of her. She at once forgot where she was, leapt up from the bed, and ran after the mouse to eat it. The indignant goddess then restored her to her original form.

¶ In the same way a bad man retains his character even if his outward appearance is altered.

THE PATIENCE OF FEAR

A bull, pursued by a lion, fled for refuge into a cave inhabited by some wild goats, which began to butt him with their horns. 'It's not because I'm afraid of *you*,' he said, 'that I put up with this, but because I'm afraid of the beast that is standing outside.'

¶ Through fear of someone stronger, people will often take the attacks of weaker men lying down.

NOTHING TO LOSE

Cantabit vacuus coram latrone viator

Two mules were travelling heavily laden, one with panniers full of money, the other with sacks crammed with barley. The one which carried the valuable load went along with his neck erect and his head in the air, shaking the bell on his collar to make it tinkle loudly, while his companion followed with a quiet, sedate step. Suddenly some bandits jumped out of an ambush. In the murderous fight that followed, the first mule received a sword-thrust and the cash was looted; but the thieves did not think the barley worth troubling about. The mule which had been robbed began to bewail his hard fate. 'For my part,' said the other, 'I am glad they thought me beneath their notice. For I have lost nothing and I have a whole skin.'

¶ The humble poor live safe; the rich are in continual peril.

HOIST WITH HER OWN PETARD

A goat and an ass were kept by the same master. The goat was jealous of the ass because he had food enough and to spare. 'Your life is one unending toil,' she said to him, 'what with turning the millstone and carrying loads. I advise you to pretend to have a fit and tumble into a hole, so that you can have a rest.' The ass took her advice, and was seriously injured by his fall. So their master sent for the veterinary surgeon and requested his help. He prescribed broth made from a goat's lung, which he said would effect a cure. So they butchered the goat to doctor the ass.

¶ To lay a trap for someone else is sometimes to become the author of your own ruin.

After driving his flock to pasture one day a goatherd noticed that it was joined by some wild goats. In the evening he drove them all to his cave. The next day he was prevented by foul weather from taking them to the usual pasture and had to attend to them indoors. He gave his own animals a ration that was just enough to save them from being famished, but he heaped the fodder generously before the newcomers in the hope of increasing his flock by domesticating them. When the weather cleared he took them all out to pasture, and as soon as they set foot on the mountains the wild goats took to their heels. The herdsman charged them with ingratitude for deserting him after the special attention he had shown them. They turned round and told him that this was precisely what had put them on their guard against him. 'We came to you only yesterday,' they said, 'and yet you treated us better than your old charges. Obviously, therefore, if others join your flock later on, you will make much of them at our expense.'

¶ We should be chary of accepting the friendly offers of people who prefer us to their old friends when we are new acquaintances. We must remember that when we become old friends they will find other new ones, and then it will be our turn to take a back seat.

ONE THING AT A TIME

Lagging behind the rest of the flock, a young goat found himself chased by a wolf. He turned to it and said: 'I know very well that you are going to make a meal of me. But I should like to die with due ceremony. Please play the flute for me to dance.' While the flute-playing and the dancing were in progress the noise brought the dogs on the scene. Chased off by them the wolf turned round and said: 'Serve me right! When I had butcher's work to do I should not have turned flute-player.'

¶ People who act without due consideration of the business in hand lose even what they have within their grasp.

A BAD WORKMAN

A sheep was being shorn clumsily. 'If it's my wool you want,' it said, 'don't cut so close. If it's my flesh you're after, kill me outright, don't torture me to death by inches.'

SOUND AND FURY SIGNIFYING NOTHING

A lion and an ass made a partnership and went out to hunt. When they came to a cave in which there were some wild goats, the lion stood at the entrance to watch for them coming out, while the ass went inside to scare them out by charging into their midst and braying. The lion caught most of them, and then the ass came out and asked if he hadn't put up a good show at driving them out. 'I give you my word,' replied the lion, 'I should have been frightened of you myself if I hadn't known you were an ass.'

¶ People who brag to those who know them must expect to be laughed at.

A man who was intending to buy an ass took one on trial and placed it along with his own asses at the manger. It turned its back on all of them save one, the laziest and greediest of the lot; it stood close beside this one and just did nothing. So the man put a halter on it and took it back to its owner, who asked if he thought that was giving it a fair trial. 'I don't want any further trial,' he answered. 'I am quite sure it is like the one that it singled out as a companion.'

❡ A man's character is judged by that of the friends whose society he takes pleasure in.

COUNTING THE COST

A wild ass which saw a tame one sunning itself went up and congratulated it on its sleek condition and the good food that it enjoyed. Later, however, he saw it with a load on its back and a driver following behind and beating it with a stick. 'I cannot congratulate you now,' he said; 'for I see you have to pay dear for having plenty to eat.'

¶ There is nothing enviable in advantages which are obtainable at the price of danger and suffering.

TOO CLEVER BY HALF

An ass crossing a river with a load of salt lost his footing and slipped into the water, so that the salt was dissolved. He was mightily pleased at finding himself relieved of his burden when he got upon his legs again. So the next time he came to a river with a load on his back, thinking that the same thing would happen if he got into the water, he let himself go under on purpose. But this time he was loaded with sponges, which absorbed so much water that he could not keep his head up and was drowned.

¶ There are men like the ass in this fable. They are taken by surprise when their own scheming lands them in disaster.

ASININE PRIDE

An ass was being driven into town with a statue of a god mounted on his back. When the passers-by did obeisance to the statue, the ass imagined that it was he to whom they showed this respect, and he was so elated that he started to bray and refused to budge a step farther. His driver, taking in the situation, laid on with his stick. 'Wretch!' he cried, 'that would be the last straw, for men to bow down to an ass.'

¶ When people boast of honours that do not rightfully belong to them, they make themselves a laughing-stock to those who know them.

AN ASS IN A LION'S SKIN

I

An ass put on a lion's skin and went about terrifying all the brute beasts. Encountering a fox, he tried to frighten it like the rest. But the fox happened to have heard him giving tongue. 'I declare,' he said, 'I should have been scared of you myself, if I had not heard you bray.'

¶ Uneducated men, who by putting on airs manage to pass for somebodies, often give themselves away because they cannot refrain from chattering.

An ass put on a lion's skin, and both men and animals took him for a lion and fled from him. But when a puff of wind stripped off the skin and left him bare, everyone ran up and began to beat him with sticks and cudgels.

¶ A poor commoner should not try to ape the style of the rich. By so doing he exposes himself to ridicule and danger; for no man can make his own what does not belong to him.

KNOW YOUR LIMITATIONS

A man owned a Maltese spaniel and an ass. He made a habit of playing with the dog, and whenever he dined out he used to bring back something to give it when it came and fawned on him. The ass was jealous; and one day it ran up to its master and frisked around him – with the result that he received a kick which made him so angry that he told his servants to drive the ass off with blows and tie it to its manger.

¶ Nature has not endowed us all with the same powers. There are things that some of us cannot do.

EVERY MAN TO HIS OWN TRADE

An ass which saw a wolf running at him, while he was grazing in a meadow, pretended to be lame. When the wolf came up and asked what made him lame, he said that he had trodden on a thorn in jumping over a fence, and advised the wolf to pull it out before eating him, so that it would not prick its mouth. The wolf fell into the trap and lifted up the ass's foot. While it was intently examining the hoof the ass kicked it in the mouth and knocked out its teeth. 'I have got what I deserved,' said the wolf in this sorry plight. 'My father taught me the trade of a butcher, and I had no business to meddle with doctoring.'

¶ Those who interfere with what does not concern them must expect to get into trouble.

ONE MASTER AS GOOD
AS ANOTHER

Poor men generally find that a change of government simply means exchanging one master for another – a truth which is illustrated in the following little anecdote.

A timid old man was grazing his donkey in a meadow when all of a sudden he was alarmed by the shouting of some enemy soldiers. 'Run for it,' he cried, 'so that they can't catch us.' But the donkey was in no hurry. 'Tell me,' said he: 'if I fall into the conqueror's hands, do you think he will make me carry a double load?' 'I shouldn't think so,' was the old man's answer. – 'Then what matter to me what master I serve as long as I only have to bear my ordinary burden?'

FOREWARNED IS FOREARMED

A farmer was confined to his homestead by bad weather. Unable to go out and find food, he began by eating his sheep; and as the storms still continued, it was the goats' turn next. Finally, since the rain did not cease, he was driven to slaughtering his plough oxen. At this the dogs, who had been watching what he did, said to each other: 'We had better make ourselves scarce. If the master doesn't spare even the oxen which share his labour, how can we expect him to keep his hands off us?'

¶ Beware above all of people who do not shrink from ill-using their friends.

EATING THE BREAD OF IDLENESS

A man trained one of his two dogs to hunt and kept the other as a house dog. The hunting dog complained bitterly because, whenever he caught any game in the chase, the other was given a share of it. 'It is not fair,' he said, 'that I should go out and have such a hard time of it, while you do nothing and live well on the fruits of my labour.' 'Well, don't blame *me*,' said the other dog. 'It is the master's fault; for he did not teach me to work myself, but only to eat what others have worked for.'

¶ It is the same with children. They cannot be blamed for being lazy if their parents bring them up in idleness.

RECKONING WITHOUT HIS HOST

A man was making ready to entertain a particular friend at dinner, and his dog invited another dog whom he knew to come and dine with him. When he arrived he stood looking at the sumptuous meal that was prepared, and his heart cried aloud for joy. 'What an unexpected treat has come my way!' he said to himself. 'I'm going to have a good feed, such a bellyful that I shan't be hungry all day tomorrow.' And all the time he kept wagging his tail to show what confidence he had in his friend's kindness. But as his tail went to and fro the cook spotted him, and immediately he seized him by the legs and threw him out of doors. He went off home howling. 'What was the dinner like?' asked one of the dogs whom he met on the way. 'There was such a lot of drink that I took too much,' he answered; 'I was so drunk that I don't even know how I got out of the house.'

¶ It is bad policy to trust those who offer to do one a good turn at someone else's expense.

THINGS ARE NOT ALWAYS WHAT
THEY SEEM

There was a dog which was fond of eating eggs. Mistaking a shell-fish for an egg one day, he opened his mouth wide and bolted it with one great gulp. The weight of it in his stomach caused him intense pain. 'Serve me right,' he said, 'for thinking that anything round must be an egg.'

¶ People who rush at things without using judgement run themselves into strange and unexpected dangers.

PROFITING BY EXPERIENCE

A dog was sleeping in front of some farm buildings when he was set upon by a wolf. In another moment he would have been devoured, but he begged the wolf not to eat him just then. 'At present,' he said, 'I am thin and lean. But if you will wait a little, my master and his family are going to celebrate a wedding. Then I shall have plenty of food and shall get fatter so that you will find me better eating.' The wolf agreed to postpone his meal and went away. Some time afterwards he returned, and finding the dog asleep on the roof of one of the buildings he called to him to come down and keep his appointment. 'If you ever catch me sleeping on the ground again,' replied the dog, 'don't wait for any wedding feast.'

¶ When a wise man has escaped from a perilous situation, he is on his guard against a similar danger for the rest of his life.

SUBSTANCE AND SHADOW

A dog was crossing over a river with a piece of meat in her mouth. Seeing her own reflection in the water she thought it was another dog with a bigger piece of meat. So she dropped her own piece and made a spring to snatch the piece that the other dog had. The result was that she had neither. She could not get the other piece because it did not exist, and her own was swept down by the current.

¶ This tale shows what happens to people who always want more than they have.

LOST TO SHAME

A dog had a way of biting people on the sly, and his master hung a bell round his neck so that everyone would know when he was about. He then started to shake his bell and show off in the market place. 'What makes you fancy yourself so?' an old bitch asked him. 'That bell of yours is not a prize for good behaviour. You are carrying it because the vicious nature you concealed so carefully has been discovered.'

¶ The vainglorious ways of impostors only serve to expose their secret sins.

TURNING THE TABLES ON
A PURSUER

A hunting dog started to chase a lion which he happened to see, but when the lion turned round and began to roar he took fright and retreated. A fox which saw him said: 'You good-for-nothing creature, you were for chasing a lion, but you couldn't stand even his roar.'

¶ There are men like the dog in this story. They are presumptuous enough to start slandering people stronger than themselves, but if their victims stand their ground they quickly sit back on their haunches.

NOT INTERESTED

An ass and a dog journeying together found a sealed paper on the ground. The ass picked it up and after breaking the seal and unfolding the paper began to read it aloud while the dog listened. It happened to be concerned with different sorts of fodder – hay, barley, and bran. Finding the lecture not at all to his taste, the dog said: 'Look a little farther down, my dear friend. If you skip a bit you may find something about meat and bones.' But the ass went through the whole of it without finding anything of the kind. 'Throw it away,' cried the dog; 'it's worthless rubbish.'

FALSE-HEARTED FAWNING

A shepherd had a huge dog to which he used to throw still-born lambs and dying sheep. One day when the flock had entered the fold he saw the dog going up to some of the sheep and fondling them lovingly. 'Hi, you there!' he cried. 'I know what you want to happen to them, and I hope it happens to you instead.'

ASLEEP WITH ONE EYE OPEN

A smith had a dog which slept while he worked but stood at his side when he ate. 'Sleepy wretch!' he cried as he threw it a bone. 'When I strike the anvil you go to bed, but when I get my teeth into action you're soon awake.'

¶ This tale is meant to pillory idle sleepyheads who live by other men's toil.

Sudden generosity may please a fool, but men of experience will not walk into such a trap.

A thief who came in the night threw a piece of bread to the house dog, to see whether it could be put off its guard by the offer of food. 'Oh ho!' said the dog. 'Are you trying to stop my mouth, so that I shan't bark to protect my master? You are very much mistaken. When you're so kind all of a sudden, I know I've got to keep wide awake and see that I don't let you get away with something.'

DOG IN THE MANGER

A dog, lying in a manger, would neither eat the barley herself nor allow the horse, which could eat it, to come near it.

ALL THE DIFFERENCE

A dog started a hare out of a bush, but, practised game-dog through he was, found himself left behind by the scampering of its hairy feet. A goat-herd laughed at him: 'Fancy a little creature like that being faster than you!' 'It's one thing,' answered the dog, 'running because you want to catch something, and quite another thing running to save your own skin.'

SOMETHING TO SQUEAL ABOUT

A pig joined a flock of sheep and grazed with them. One day the shepherd laid hands on it, and it began to squeal and struggle. The sheep found fault with it for crying out. 'He takes hold of us often,' they said, 'and we don't make a fuss.' 'Yes, but it's a different thing his laying hold of you,' said the pig. 'He only wants your wool or your milk, but it's my flesh he's after.'

¶ A man has something to shout about when it is his life and not just his property that is in danger.

SCAMPED WORK

A sow and a bitch were disputing which of them brought forth her young more easily. The bitch claimed that she welped more quickly than any other quadruped. 'That's all very well,' said the sow, 'but allow me to point out that your puppies are blind when they are born.'

¶ Things are judged not by the speed but by the perfection with which they are done.

A PERSON OF NO IMPORTANCE

A prolonged and desperate fight was going on between some dolphins and whales when a tiny sea-gudgeon came to the surface and attempted to reconcile them. It was dismissed with this retort from one of the dolphins: 'We would rather go on fighting till we kill one another than have *you* mediating between us.'

¶ Some nobodies think they are somebody when they interfere in a row.

DESPISE NOT A FEEBLE FOLK

A hare pursued by an eagle was in sore need of succour. It happened that the only creature in sight was a beetle, to which he appealed for help. The beetle bade him take courage, and on seeing the eagle approach called upon her to spare the suppliant who had sought its protection. But the eagle, despising so tiny a creature, devoured the hare before its eyes. The beetle bore her a grudge for this, and was continually on the watch to see where she made her nest. Every time she laid eggs, it flew up to the nest, rolled the eggs out, and broke them. Driven from pillar to post, the eagle at last took refuge with Zeus and begged him to give her – his own sacred bird – a safe place to hatch her chicks. Zeus allowed her to lay her eggs in his lap. But the beetle saw her; so it made a ball of dung, and flying high above Zeus dropped it into his lap. Without stopping to think, Zeus got up to shake it off, and tipped out the eggs. Ever since that time, they say eagles do not nest during the season when beetles are about.

¶ This fable is a warning against holding anyone in contempt. You must remember that even the feeblest man, if you trample him in the mud, can find a way some day to pay you out.

EXAMPLE IS BETTER THAN
PRECEPT

A mother crab was telling her son not to walk sideways or rub its sides against the wet rock. 'All right, mother,' it replied; 'since you want to teach me, walk straight yourself. I'll watch you and copy you.'

¶ Fault-finders ought to walk straight and live straight before they set about instructing others.

PROOF POSITIVE

A cicada sat chirping in a tall tree, and a fox which wanted to devour it thought out a plan. He stood facing it and spoke with admiration of its beautiful voice. Then he asked it to come down. He wanted, he said, to see how big it was, having heard what a loud voice it had. But the cicada did not fall into the trap. It broke off a leaf and dropped it, and the fox darted forwards, never doubting that it was the insect. 'You were wrong, my friend,' said the cicada, 'if you thought I would come down. I have been on my guard against foxes ever since the day when I saw cicadas' wings in a fox's droppings.'

❡ Sensible men learn wisdom from their neighbour's misadventures.

BEARDING THE LION

A gnat went up to a lion and said: 'I'm not afraid of you. You can't do anything more than I can. If you think you can, then tell me what it is. Scratch with your claws, perhaps, and bite with your teeth? Any woman who has a fight with her husband does as much. I am far stronger than you, and I'm ready for a battle if you are.' And sounding its trumpet the gnat fastened on him, biting the hairless part of his face round the nostrils. The lion kept tearing himself with his own claws, until in the end he cried off from the fight. With another blast on its trumpet the victorious gnat set up a hum of triumph and flew away. But it got entangled in a spider's web, and while it was being devoured it lamented the irony of fate which allowed a creature capable of doing battle with the strongest animals to be destroyed by such an insignificant thing as a spider.

BENEATH NOTICE

A gnat alighted on a bull's horn. After it had stayed there a long time and felt like moving on, it asked the bull if he would like it to go now. 'I didn't notice when you came,' replied the bull, 'and I shall not notice if you go.'

¶ Some people are so feeble that it makes no differ-ence whether they are there or not, because they can do neither good nor harm.

THE WAGES OF MALICE

The bees grudged their honey to men because they regarded it as their own property. So they went to Zeus and prayed him to grant them the power of stinging to death anyone who approached their combs. Zeus was so angry with them for their ill-nature, that he condemned them not only to lose their stings whenever they used them on anyone, but to forfeit their lives as well.

¶ This fable is an apt censure of people who indulge their ill-will even at the cost of injury to themselves.

WHY THE ANT IS A THIEF

The first ant began life as a human being. He was a farmer who, not content with the fruit of his own labours, kept casting envious eyes on his neighbours' produce and stealing it. His greed made Zeus so angry that he transformed him into the insect which we call the ant. But even when his form was altered his character remained unchanged. To this day he goes to and fro in the fields collecting other people's wheat and barley and storing it up for himself.

¶ This fable is meant to show that even the severest punishment does not change the original character of a bad man.

GO TO THE ANT, THOU SLUGGARD

I

An ant spent all the summer running about the fields and collecting grains of wheat and barley to store for the winter. A beetle which saw it expressed amazement at its industry in working hard even during the season when other creatures had a holiday and rested from their labours. At the time, the ant held its peace. But later on, when winter set in and the rain washed away the dung, the beetle came famished with hunger and begged the ant for a share of its food. 'You should have worked,' the ant replied, 'when I was hard at work, instead of sneering at me. If you had done so, you would not be short of food now.'

¶ The ant teaches men to take thought for the morrow in a season of abundance, lest, when times change, they suffer dire distress.

GO TO THE ANT, THOU SLUGGARD

2

It was winter-time; the ants' store of grain had got wet and they were laying it out to dry. A hungry cicada asked them to give it something to eat. 'Why did you not gather food in the summer, like us?' they said. 'I hadn't time,' it replied; 'I was busy making sweet music.' The ants laughed at it. 'Very well,' they said; 'since you piped in summer, now dance in winter.'

¶ In everything beware of negligence, if you want to escape distress and danger.

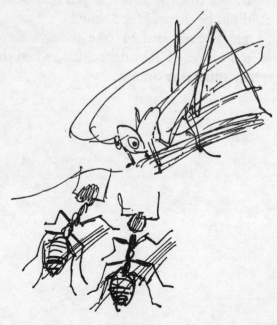

ONE GOOD TURN DESERVES ANOTHER

A thirsty ant which had crawled into a rivulet was carried away by the current. A dove, seeing it in danger of drowning, broke off a twig and threw it into the water. The ant got onto it and was saved. Later, a fowler came with his limed sticks placed in position to catch the dove. When the ant saw him it stung his foot, and the pain made him drop the sticks, which frightened the dove away.

THE AXE IS LAID UNTO THE ROOT
OF THE TREES

A fir-tree and a thorn-bush were arguing with each other, and the fir was singing its own praises. 'I am beautiful and tall,' it said to the thorn, 'and useful for making temple roofs and ships. How can you compare yourself with me?' 'But remember the axes and saws which cut you,' was the reply, 'and then you will wish you were a thorn-bush.'

¶ No one should be vainglorious in this life; for it is insignificant people who live most safely.

BOWING BEFORE THE STORM

A reed and an olive tree were disputing about their strength and their powers of quiet endurance. When the reed was reproached by the olive with being weak and easily bent by every wind, it answered not a word. Soon afterwards a strong wind began to blow. The reed, by letting itself be tossed about and bent by the gusts, weathered the storm without difficulty; but the olive, which resisted it, was broken by its violence.

¶ The moral is that people should accept the situation in which they find themselves and yield to superior force. This is better than kicking against the pricks.

A FABLED FLOWER THAT
FADES NOT

An amaranth grew beside a rose. 'How lovely you are,' it said to the rose, 'and how desirable in the eyes of gods and men! I felicitate you on your beauty and your fragrance.' 'But my life,' replied the rose, 'is a short one; even if no one cuts me, I wither. You continue to bloom and remain always as fresh as you are now.'

¶ It is better to be content with little and live long than to enjoy a short spell of luxury and then exchange it for misfortune, or even for death.

THE GENTLE ART OF PERSUASION

The north wind and the sun were disputing which was the stronger, and agreed to acknowledge as the victor whichever of them could strip a traveller of his clothing. The wind tried first. But its violent gusts only made the man hold his clothes tightly around him, and when it blew harder still the cold made him so uncomfortable that he put on an extra wrap. Eventually the wind got tired of it and handed him over to the sun. The sun shone first with a moderate warmth, which made the man take off his top-coat. Then it blazed fiercely, till, unable to stand the heat, he stripped and went off to bathe in a near-by river.

¶ This fable shows that very often persuasion is more effective than force.

Winter scoffed tauntingly at Spring. 'When you appear,' he said, 'no one stays still a moment longer. Some are off to meadows or woods: they must needs be picking lilies and other flowers, twiddling roses round in their fingers to examine them, or sticking them in their hair. Others go on board ship and cross the wide ocean, maybe, to visit men of other lands; and not a man troubles himself any more about gales or downpours of rain. Now I am like a ruler or dictator. I bid men look not up to the sky but down to the earth with fear and trembling, and sometimes they have to resign themselves to staying indoors all day.' 'Yes,' replied Spring, 'and therefore men would gladly be rid of you. But with me it is different. They think my name very lovely – yes, by Zeus, the loveliest name of all names. When I am absent they cherish my memory, and when I reappear they are full of rejoicing.'

EASILY REMEDIED

The rivers gathered together and made a complaint against the sea. 'Why,' they said, 'when we enter your waters fresh and fit to drink, do you make us salt and undrinkable?' Hearing itself thus blamed, the sea replied: 'Don't come: then you won't become salt.'

¶ This fable satirizes people who make unreasonable accusations against those who are really their benefactors.

MARCHING ON THE STOMACH

The belly and the feet were arguing with each other about their strength. The feet kèpt on saying that they must be much stronger than the belly, because they actually carried it about. 'That's all very well, my friends,' replied the belly; 'but if I stop supplying you with nourishment you won't be able to carry me.'

THE IMPIOUS HUCKSTER

A man once made a wooden statue of Hermes and took it to market to sell. As no buyer came forward, he tried to attract one by shouting aloud that he was offering for sale a god who would confer blessings on a man and make him prosper. 'Oh, are you?' said a bystander. 'If he is all you say he is, why do you want to sell him? You would show more sense if you kept him and profited by his help.' 'But it's ready money *I* need,' the man replied, 'and it generally takes him a long time to put anything into one's pocket.'

¶ The man in this story was one of those who will stoop to anything in their greed for gain and never give a thought to the gods.

WHO ART THOU THAT JUDGEST?

A man who saw a ship sink with all hands protested against the injustice of the gods: because there was one impious person on board, he said, they had destroyed the innocent as well. As he spoke he was bitten by one of a swarm of ants which happened to be there; and, though only one had attacked him, he trampled on them all. At this Hermes appeared and smote him with his staff, saying: 'Will you not allow the gods to judge men as you judge ants?'

¶ Let not a man blaspheme against God in the day of calamity, but let him rather examine his own faults.

WHAT A PIECE OF WORK IS MAN!

According to tradition the animals were fashioned before man, and Zeus endowed them with various powers, such as strength, and swiftness of foot or wing. Man, standing naked before him, complained that he alone was left without any such endowment. 'You do not appreciate what has been given you,' said Zeus. 'You have received the greatest gift of all – the gift of reason, which is all-powerful in heaven and on earth, stronger than the strong, swifter than the swift.' This made man realize what had been vouchsafed him, and he departed with adoration and thanks-giving.

¶ Although all men have been favoured by God with the gift of reason, some are insensible of this privilege and choose rather to envy creatures which lack the faculties of perception and rational thought.

A RASH PRAYER ANSWERED

A cowherd missed a calf from the herd that he was pasturing and could not find it anywhere. He vowed to sacrifice a kid to Zeus if he caught the thief. On going into a wood he saw a lion devouring the calf, and, lifting his hands to heaven in terror, cried out: 'Lord Zeus, I promised before to offer up a kid on your altar if I discovered the thief; now, I will sacrifice a bull to get out of reach of his claws.'

¶ People who are in trouble will often pray for things which, when they get them, they want to be rid of.

DIRT CHEAP

Hermes wanted to find out how highly men valued him, and taking the shape of a human being he went to a sculptor's workshop. On seeing a statue of Zeus he inquired its price. 'A drachma,' the man said. With a laugh Hermes went on to ask the same question about one representing Hera, and was told that it was more expensive than the other. At length he noticed a statue of himself. Thinking that his dual character as the messenger of Zeus and the God of Gain must cause him to be held in high esteem by mankind, he asked: 'And how much is the Hermes?' 'Oh,' replied the sculptor, 'if you buy the other two, I'll throw him in for nothing.'

¶ This story ridicules conceited people who are held in no account by others.

A CARTLOAD OF MISCHIEF

Once upon a time Hermes was driving all over the world a cart stuffed with falsehoods, wickedness, and deceit, distributing a little of his load in each country. But when he came to the land of the Arabs, it is said, the cart suddenly broke in pieces, and the inhabitants plundered its contents as if they were valuable merchandise, so that there was nothing left for Hermes to carry elsewhere.

¶ The Arabs are the greatest liars and deceivers on earth. Their tongues know not the truth.

WHY GIANTS ARE BOOBIES

After Zeus had fashioned men he told Hermes to put intelligence into them. Hermes made a vessel for measuring it and poured an equal quantity into every man. It was enough to fill the little men full, so that they became wise. But the dram was too small to percolate all through the bodies of the big men; so they turned our rather stupid.

ALL LOST SAVE HOPE

Zeus packed all the good things of life in a jar, put a lid on it, and left it in the care of a certain man. Itching to know what was inside, the man lifted the lid. The contents immediately flew up into the air and departed from earth to heaven. Only Hope remained – for she was shut in when he clapped the lid on again.

¶ Mankind have only Hope to promise them recovery of the blessings they have lost.

ROOM FOR IMPROVEMENT

Zeus made a bull, Prometheus a man, and Athena a house; and they chose Momus to judge their handiwork. He was so jealous of it that he began to find fault with everything. Zeus, he said, had made a mistake in not putting the bull's eyes in its horns, to enable it to see what it was butting. Prometheus' man should have had his mind attached to the outside of his body; then his thoughts would have been visible, so that wickedness could not be hidden. As for Athena, she ought to have mounted her house on wheels, so that one could move without any trouble if a rogue came to live next door. Zeus was angered by this display of malice and exiled Momus from Olympus.

¶ Nothing is so good that some fault cannot be found with it.

HONESTY IS THE BEST POLICY

A man who was cutting wood on a riverside lost his axe in the water. There was no help for it; so he sat down on the bank and began to cry. Hermes appeared and inquired what was the matter. Feeling sorry for the man, he dived into the river, brought up a gold axe, and asked him if that was the one he had lost. When the woodcutter said that it was not, Hermes dived again and fetched up a silver one. The man said that was not his either. So he went down a third time and came up with the woodcutter's own axe. 'That's the right one,' he said; and Hermes was so delighted with his honesty that he made him a present of the other two axes as well. When the wood/man rejoined his mates and told them his experience, one of them thought he would bring off a similar coup. He went to the river, deliberately threw his axe into it, and then sat down and wept. Hermes appeared again; and on hearing the cause of his tears, he dived in, produced a gold axe as before, and asked if it was the one that had been lost. 'Yes, it is indeed,' the man joyfully exclaimed. The god was so shocked at his unblushing impudence, that, far from giving him the gold axe, he did not even restore his own to him.

¶ This fable shows that heaven is as determined to thwart a rogue as it is ready to help an honest man.

THE FAULT, DEAR BRUTUS, IS NOT IN
OUR STARS, BUT IN OURSELVES

A man who was tired after a long journey threw himself down on the edge of a well and went to sleep. He was in imminent danger of tumbling in, when Fortune appeared and woke him. 'If you had fallen in, my friend,' she said, 'instead of blaming your own imprudence you would have blamed me.'

¶ Many people who meet with misfortune through their own fault put the blame on the gods.

NO RESPITE

A man to whom a friend had entrusted some money was trying to rob him of it. When his friend challenged him to deny the debt on oath, he thought it safest to go away into the country. On reaching the gates, however, he saw a lame man leaving the town, and asked him who he was and where he was going. 'Oath is my name,' replied the man, 'and I am going to punish perjurers.'

'And how long is it usually before you return to a city?'

'Forty years, or sometimes thirty.'

The embezzler hesitated no longer, the very next day he solemnly swore that he had never had the money. But soon he found himself face to face with the lame man, who haled him off to be thrown from a high rock. The culprit started to whine. 'You said it would be thirty years before you returned,' he complained, 'and you have not let me escape for a single day.' 'Yes,' replied the other, 'when someone is determined to provoke me, I come back the very same day.'

¶ No man can tell when God's punishment will fall upon the wicked.

WHY SOME MEN ARE LOUTISH
BRUTES

On the orders of Zeus, Prometheus fashioned men and beasts. Seeing that the beasts were much more numerous, Zeus commanded him to unmake some of them and turn them into men, and he did as he was told. But those who had not originally been fashioned as men, even though they now had a human form, still had the minds of beasts.

A CITY OF LIES

Travelling through a desert a man saw a woman standing all alone with eyes bent on the ground.

'Who are you?' he asked.

'I am Truth,' she answered.

'And why have you left the town to live in the desert.'

'Because times have changed,' she said. 'In days gone by, lying was confined to a few. But nowadays whenever you converse with people you find they are all liars.'

❡ Human life is a vile and wretched thing, when falsehood is honoured above truth.

THE EYE-DOCTOR

An old woman whose sight was bad offered a doctor a fee to cure her. He treated her with ointment, and after each application, while her eyes were closed, he kept stealing her possessions one by one. When he had removed them all he said that the cure was completed and demanded the fee agreed upon. The woman, however, refused to pay; so he summoned her before the magistrates. Her defence was that she promised to pay the money if he cured her sight; but after his treatment it got worse than it was to start with. 'Before he began,' she said, 'I could see all the things in the house, and now I can't see anything.'

¶ Some people are so intent on dishonest gain that they fail to see when they are providing proof of their own guilt.

INCURABLE

A woman whose husband was a drunkard devised a plan to cure him of this failing. She waited till he was dead drunk – blind to the world – and then, hoisting him on her shoulders, she carried him to the cemetery and dumped him there. When she thought he had had time to sleep it off, she went back and knocked at the gate. 'Who's there?' he called; and she answered that she was bringing an offering of food for the dead. 'I don't want to eat, man,' he said; 'bring something to drink. Damn your food! Drink's the stuff for me!' At this the woman beat her breast and cried: 'Woe is me! Much good I've done with all my scheming! Far from teaching you a lesson, it's made you worse than ever. Your weakness has become second nature with you.'

¶ This tale is a warning against persisting in evil practices. A time will come when, even if one wants to, one cannot break the habit.

A COMMON CHEAT

There was once a sorceress who, professing to sell charms and the means of appeasing divine wrath, always had plenty of clients and made a good living out of them. For these practices she was charged with heresy, arraigned, and condemned to death. When she was being led out of court an onlooker said: 'Since you claim to be able to avert the anger of the gods, my good woman, how comes it that you cannot even prevail upon men?'

¶ Such is the trickery of vagabond women who, pretending to work miracles, are proved incapable of doing what is comparatively easy.

A WARNING AGAINST CALUMNY

A bandit had killed a man on the highway. When he was pursued by the passers-by, he left his victim covered with blood and fled. Some people coming in the opposite direction asked him what had stained his hands. He replied that he had just climbed down a mulberry tree. While he was speaking his pursuers arrived, laid hold of him, and hung him on a mulberry tree with a stake driven through his body. 'I don't mind helping to put you to death,' said the tree to him. 'You committed a murder yourself, and then tried to wipe off the blood on me.'

¶ Even a naturally good man, if you slander his character, will often show himself towards you as black as you have painted him.

A PROPHET WITHOUT KNOWLEDGE

A fortune-teller was sitting in the market-place and doing good business. Suddenly a man came and told him that the door of his house had been wrenched from its hinges and all his possessions carried off. He jumped up and with a cry of consternation ran to see what had happened. A bystander who was watching him said: 'You profess to foretell what is going to befall other people, but you did not foresee your own misfortune.'

¶ This fable exposes the folly of men who mismanage their own lives, yet claim to possess foresight in matters which do not concern them.

TRUTH TURNED LIAR

Two boys went together to a shop to buy meat. While the butcher's back was turned one of them pilfered some offal and thrust it into the other's pocket. On looking round the man missed it and charged the boys with stealing it. The one who had taken it swore that he had not got it, and the one who had it swore that he had not taken it. The shopman, who saw through their trick, said: 'You may cheat *me* by swearing deceitfully, but you won't cheat the gods.'

¶ Perjury is not made any less wicked by quibbling.

THE SWINDLER

A man who was making a long journey vowed to dedicate to Hermes one half of anything he found on the way. One day he found a wallet, which he picked up, not doubting that it contained money. But when he shook out the contents, there was nothing but some almonds and dates. After eating them he took the shells of the almonds and the stones of the dates, and laid them on an altar. 'I have discharged my vow, Hermes,' he said; 'for I have given you as your share the outsides and the insides of what I found.'

¶ This fable portrays the money-grubber who is so greedy that he cheats even gods.

SPARE THE ROD AND SPOIL
THE CHILD

A schoolboy stole his classmate's writing-tablet and took it to his mother, who instead of reproving him praised him. Another time he brought her a stolen cloak, for which she praised him still more highly. When he grew up to be a young man he ventured on more serious thefts. But one day he was caught in the act, whereupon his hands were tied behind his back and he was led off to execution. His mother went with him, beating her breast, and he said that he wanted to whisper something in her ear. The moment she went up to him, he took the lobe of her ear in his teeth and bit it. She reproached him for his unfilial conduct: not content with the other crimes he had committed, he had now done grievous bodily harm to his mother. 'The time when you should have reproved me,' he said, 'was when I committed my first theft and brought you the tablet I had stolen. Then I should not have ended up in the hands of the executioner.'

❡ Impunity leads offenders on from bad to worse.

THE CHARLATAN

A cobbler, who was such a bad workman that he was almost starving, went to a place where he was not known and set up as a doctor. He sold some stuff which he pretended was an antidote against poison, and he was such a ready-tongued trickster that he made quite a reputation for himself. One day, when a favourite servant of the king's was lying seriously ill, the king sent for the quack and decided to test his skill. Calling for a cup, he poured out some water, told the quack to put in his antidote, and then pretended to add some poison to it. 'Now drink it,' he said, 'and I will pay you well.' The fear of death made the man confess the truth – that he knew nothing of medicine and owed his fame to the stupidity of the mob. The king assembled his people and told them the whole story. 'Do you think madness could go further?' he asked. 'You do not hesitate to entrust your lives to a man whom nobody trusted to make shoes for his feet.'

¶ Am I not right in thinking that there are many whom the cap fits – people whose folly enables impudent imposters to make money?

GOD HELPS THOSE WHO HELP THEMSELVES

A rich Athenian was on a voyage with other passengers, when a violent storm blew up and capsized the ship. All the rest tried to swim ashore, but the Athenian kept calling on Athena and promising her lavish offerings if he escaped. One of his shipwrecked companions, as he swam past, shouted to him: 'Don't leave it all to Athena; use your arms as well.'

¶ That is what we should all do. Besides invoking the aid of heaven we must think and act for ourselves.

THE BURNER BURNT

A fox had angered a farmer by the damage that it did. So when he caught it he thought he would make it pay dearly. He tied some tow soaked in oil to its tail and set fire to it. But some god made the fox go into its captor's corn-fields, which were ready for reaping, and all he could do was to run after it, lamenting the loss of his harvest.

¶ This story is a lesson in humanity and a warning against uncontrolled rage, which often does serious harm to those who give way to it.

TREASURE TROVE

A farmer who was dying wanted his sons to become good agriculturalists. He summoned them and said: 'I, my boys, am about to leave this world. You must search for what I have hidden in the vineyard. You will find there all I have to give you.' They thought there was a treasure buried somewhere in the vine-yard, and after their father was dead they dug every inch of the soil. There was no hidden treasure to be found, but the vines were so well dug that they yielded a bumper crop.

¶ This story teaches us that the fruits of toil are man's best treasure.

UNITY IS STRENGTH

A farmer whose sons were always at loggerheads tried to persuade them to mend their ways, but found that no words made any impression on them. So he decided to give them an object-lesson. He made them bring a bundle of sticks, and started by giving them the bundle as it was and telling them to break the sticks. Try as they would they could not. Then he untied the bundle and handed them the sticks one at a time, so that they could break them easily. 'It will be the same with you, my children,' he said. 'As long as you agree together no enemy can overcome you; if you quarrel, you will fall an easy prey.'

¶ Divided, men are vulnerable; it is union that makes them strong.

A MOUNTAIN OUT OF A MOLEHILL

Travelling along a narrow path, Heracles saw something on the ground that looked like an apple, and put his foot on it to crush it. But it became twice as large as it had been; whereupon he stamped on it still harder and hit it with his club. It expanded to such a size that it blocked the path. Heracles threw away his club and stood still in amazement. Then Athena appeared before him. 'That will do, brother,' she said. 'This thing is the spirit of strife and contention. So long as no one provokes it, it stays as it was at first; but if you fight it, look how it swells.'

¶ It is plain for all to see that fighting and quarrelling are the cause of untold harm.

MOTE AND BEAM

Once upon a time when Prometheus fashioned men he hung two bags from their necks, one in front of them, filled with other people's defects, and one behind their backs containing their own defects. Thus men can see their fellows' faults a mile away, but can never perceive their own.

¶ This story satirizes the busybody who, blind as regards his own affairs, concerns himself about other men's.

A FRIEND IN NEED IS A
FRIEND INDEED

Two friends were travelling together when a bear suddenly appeared. One of them climbed up a tree in
time and remained there hidden. The other, seeing
that he would be caught in another moment, lay
down on the ground and pretended to be dead. When
the bear put its muzzle to him and smelt him all over,
he held his breath – for it is said that a bear will not
touch a corpse. After it had gone away, the other man
came down from his tree and asked his friend what
the bear had whispered in his ear. 'It told me,' he
replied, 'not to travel in future with friends who do
not stand by one in peril.'

❡ Genuine friends are proved by adversity.

SHARE AND SHARE ALIKE

Two men were journeying together when one of them noticed an axe lying on the ground. 'We have had a lucky find,' said his companion. 'Don't say "We",' replied the other; 'say "You have had a find".' Shortly afterwards the people who had lost the axe came up with them, and the man who had it, seeing the owners in pursuit, said: 'We are done for.' 'Don't say "We",' his companion answered; 'say "I am done for" – since when you found the axe you would not let me share possession of it.'

¶ If we do not give our friends a share of our good fortune, they will not be faithful to us in adversity.

MUCH WANTS MORE

Hermes gave to a particularly pious worshipper a goose that laid golden eggs. But the man was too impatient to wait for wealth to come in driblets, and thinking that the bird's inside must be solid gold he made haste to kill it. Not only were his hopes disappointed, but he got no more golden eggs. For he found nothing in the goose but ordinary flesh and blood.

¶ In their greed for more, grasping people often throw away what they have already.

MEMENTO MORI

A ship set sail with some passengers aboard, and on reaching the open sea it was overtaken by an unusually violent storm and was on the point of sinking. One after another the passengers began to tear their clothes and call upon their country's gods with groaning and lamentation, promising to make thank-offerings if they escaped. Eventually the storm abated and calm returned once more. Then they started to make merry, dancing and jumping for joy at their unlooked-for deliverance from peril. The pilot remained phlegmatic through it all. 'Let us not forget, my friends,' he said, 'in the midst of our rejoicing, that we may run into bad weather again.'

¶ Do not be over-much elated by good fortune. Remember how easily it can change.

WHERE YOUR TREASURE IS, THERE
WILL YOUR HEART BE ALSO

A miser sold all his possessions, made an ingot of the gold that he got for them, and hid it in a certain spot, where his own heart and thoughts were buried with it. Every day he came to gloat over his treasure. A labourer who had watched him guessed his secret, dug up the gold and carried it away; and when the miser came and found the hole empty he began to lament and pluck out his hair. A passer-by who saw him inquired the cause of his grief, and said: 'Do not be so downcast, sir. Even when you had the gold you might as well not have had it. Take a stone instead and put it in the earth, and imagine that you have the gold there. That will serve the same purpose. For as far as I can see, even when it was there you did not make any use of the gold that you possessed.'

¶ Possession without enjoyment is nothing.

SEEING IS BELIEVING

An athlete was always being called a weakling by his compatriots. So he went abroad for a time; and on his return he boasted of the many feats he had performed in various countries, and especially of a jump which he had made at Rhodes – a jump such as no Olympic victor could equal. 'I can prove it by the testimony of eye-witnesses,' he said, 'if any of the people who were present ever come here.' At this one of the bystanders said: 'If what you say is true, my man, you don't need witnesses. The place where you stand will do as well as Rhodes. Let us see the jump.'

¶ The point of this story is that it is a waste of words to talk about something which can easily be put to the proof.

PLUCKED CLEAN

A man whose hair was turning grey had two mistresses, one young and the other old. The old one was ashamed of having a younger man make love to her, and when he came to her she kept pulling out the black hairs from his head. The young woman, who did not like the idea of having an old man for a lover, used to pull out his grey hairs. So between them they ended by making him completely bald.

¶ Ill-assorted companions never come by any good.

BLIND MAN'S TOUCH

There was once a blind man, who, when any living creature was put into his hands, could tell what it was by feeling it. But one time, when someone handed him a wolf-cub, he could not make up his mind. 'I don't know,' he said after feeling it, 'whether it is the young of a wolf or a fox or some other such animal. But I do know this much, that it is no fit company for a flock of sheep.'

¶ In the same way a man's evil nature can often be recognized from his physical attributes.

OUT OF THE FRYING-PAN INTO
THE FIRE

An industrious widow used to rouse her slave girls at cockcrow to start work. In the end they were so worn out with fatigue that they decided to wring the neck of the rooster, imagining that he was responsible for all the trouble by waking their mistress before daylight. But their action only landed them in worse misfortune; for now that she no longer had the cock to tell her the time, the mistress made them get up and set to work even earlier.

¶ Many people's troubles are of their own devising.

BRAVE TALK

A huntsman, searching for a lion's tracks, asked a woodman if he had seen them and if he knew where its lair was. The man said he would show him the lion itself. At this the huntsman turned pale with fear and his teeth chattered. 'I am only looking for its trail,' he said, 'not for the lion.'

¶ This story is meant to show up the braggadocio of the coward whose boldness is in words and not in deeds.

BUSINESS FIRST

The orator Demades was once addressing the people of Athens, and since they paid little attention to his speech he asked for permission to tell them a fable of Aesop. On obtaining their consent he began: 'Demeter was travelling in company with a swallow and an eel. When they reached the bank of a river, the swallow flew up into the air and the eel plunged into the water.' At this point he stopped. 'Well,' they asked, 'and what about Demeter?' 'She is angry with you,' he said, 'because you disregard affairs of state and are all ears for Aesop's fables.'

❡ It is thoughtless folly when men neglect important business for the sake of pleasure.

HATING UNTO DEATH

Two men who hated each other were on the same ship, one sitting in the stern, the other in the bows. A storm came on, and when the ship was on the point of sinking the man in the stern asked the steersman which part of the ship would go under water first. On being told that the bows would go first, 'I do not mind dying myself,' he said, 'if I can see my enemy die before me.'

¶ Many men do not care what happens to themselves, so long as they see their enemies suffer first.

THE UNGODLY INCREASE IN RICHES

When Heracles, promoted to the rank of deity, was entertained at Zeus' table, he greeted each one of the gods very graciously. But last of all Plutus came in, whereupon Heracles bent his head down and turned away. In surprise, Zeus asked him why, after welcoming all the others with such pleasure, he looked askance at Plutus. 'Well,' said Heracles, 'it is because, when I lived among men, I generally saw him keeping bad company.'

❡ This fable reminds us that riches are a gift of fortune that may come to a man of evil character.

FALSELY ACCUSED

A quack doctor was attending a sick man. All the other physicians had said that although his illness would be a long one he was in no danger. But the quack told him to settle up all his affairs. 'You will not last beyond tomorrow,' he said; and with this warning he left him.

After some time the sick man got up and went out, pale and only just able to walk. 'Good morning,' said the doctor on meeting him; 'and how are they getting on in the Underworld?' 'Oh, they are quiet enough,' he replied, 'having had a good drink of water of the Lethe. But the other day Death and Hades were uttering dreadful threats against all the doctors because they will not let sick men die, and they were drawing up a black list of them. They were going to put your name on it, but I went down on my knees and begged you off. I swore that whoever said you were a real doctor had libelled you.'

¶ This tale is meant to pillory ignorant quacks whose only learning is the trick of making plausible speeches.

ONE SWALLOW DOES NOT MAKE
A SUMMER

A young rake had wasted his inheritance and had nothing left but a cloak. Seeing a swallow which had arrived before the usual season, he thought that summer had come and that he did not need the cloak any longer. So he took it and sold it like all the rest. But afterwards wintry weather set in with a keen frost, and as he was walking one day he saw the swallow frozen to death. 'Miserable creature,' he said; 'you have destroyed both yourself and me.'

¶ It is always dangerous to choose the wrong time for doing a thing.

FAVOURABLE OMENS

A patient, on being questioned by his doctor about his condition, answered that he had had an unpleasantly heavy sweat. 'That's good,' said the doctor. The next time he was asked how he was, he complained of a shivering-fit that had nearly shaken him to pieces. 'That's good too,' was the doctor's comment. At this third visit, he inquired once more about the man's symptoms and was told that he had had diarrhoea. 'Good again,' he said, and took himself off. When one of the patient's relatives came to see him and asked how he was getting on, 'Well, if you want to know,' he replied, 'I've had so many good symptoms that I'm just about dead.'

¶ It often happens that our neighbours not knowing where the shoe pinches us, congratulate us on the very things which we ourselves find hardest to bear.

LA FORZA DEL DESTINO

A timid old man had an only son, a brave lad who was passionately fond of hunting. Having dreamed that he saw him killed by a lion, the father was afraid that the dream was a vision of what was destined actually to happen. To prevent its coming true, therefore, he built a splendid hall raised high above the ground and kept his son there under guard. To amuse him the hall was decorated with pictures of all sorts of animals, including a lion; but the sight of them only made him more miserable. One day he stood in front of the lion and cried: 'Curse you! It is because of you and my father's lying dream that I am mewed up here like a woman. How can I pay you out?' And as he spoke he struck his hand against the wall as though he would knock out the lion's eye. A splinter went in under his nail, setting up acute pain and inflammation right down to the groin. Then a high fever supervened, from which he quickly died. So although it was but a painted picture, the lion had caused the boy's death, and his father's ingenious plan proved vain.

¶ A man should resign himself to his fate with patience and courage; for no artifice can deliver him from it.

AN UNSEASONABLE REPROOF

A boy was in danger of being drowned while bathing in a river. Seeing a traveller on the bank, he called to him for help; but the man started to lecture him on his rashness. 'Rescue me now,' cried the boy; 'you can lecture me later on when I am safe.'

⁋ This story is meant as a warning to those whose conduct gives others a pretext for treating them unkindly.

USE IS EVERYTHING

A well-to-do man came to live next door to a tanner's yard. Unable to endure the foul smell, he kept urging the tanner to remove elsewhere; but the tanner always put him off, saying that he would move a little later on. This happened so often that in course of time the man got used to the smell and stopped worrying his neighbour.

¶ When one grows accustomed to them, even disagreeable things become less trying.

LEARNING BY BITTER EXPERIENCE

A shepherd, while pasturing his flock on the shore, looked at the calm sea and decided to make a voyage as a trader. So he sold his sheep, bought a quantity of dates, and set sail. But a violent storm arose, which threatened to sink his ship, and even after jettisoning the whole of his cargo it took him all his time to bring the empty ship safely to land. Long afterwards, a passer-by drew his attention to the stillness of the sea, which happened just then to be motionless. 'Ah, my good sir,' said the shepherd, 'I expect it wants some more dates. That is why it looks so quiet.'

CRYING WOLF TOO OFTEN

There was a shepherd who was fond of playing practical jokes. He would drive his flock some distance from the village and then shout to the villagers for help, saying that wolves had attacked his sheep. Two or three times the inhabitants came rushing out in alarm – and then went back with the shepherd laughing at them. Eventually, however, some wolves really came. They got between the shepherd and his flock and he called the neighbours to aid him. But they thought he was up to his usual trick and did not bother their heads about him. So he lost his sheep.

¶ A scaremonger gains nothing by raising false alarms. He merely makes people disbelieve him when he does speak the truth.

A PHILOSOPHIC BALDPATE

A bald man, who wore a wig, was riding one day, when a puff of wind blew the wig off, at which the bystanders guffawed. Reining in his horse, he said: 'It is not surprising that I cannot keep hair which is not mine on my head, since its proper owner, on whose head it grew, could not keep it there.'

¶ Let no man be cast down by the accidents which befall him. What Nature did not give us at our birth can never be a permanent possession. Naked we came into the world, and naked shall we leave it.

FRIENDS INDEED

The name of friendship is often on men's lips, but loyal friends are few and far between.

A small house was being built for Socrates – a man whose fate I would willingly share if I might share his glory, whose ill-fame while he lived was a small price to pay for being judged guiltless now that he is dust and ashes. A passer-by made the obvious sort of remark that people do make: 'Fancy a man like you building such a poky house!' 'I only hope,' said Socrates, 'that I can find enough true friends to fill it.'

THE RIDDLE OF A WILL

One man is often of more use than a whole crowd of people. To prove which, I will set the following short story on record for posterity.

A man died and left three daughters. One was a beauty who made eyes at men to ensnare them; another was a thrifty peasant, a good wool-spinner; the third was a tippler, and very ugly. The old man's will appointed the mother his trustee, directing her to divide his whole fortune equally between the three girls, but in such a manner that 'they should not have possession or enjoyment of the property bequeathed to them.' Another clause required that, 'as soon as they should have ceased to possess the property which they received, they should each pay one thousand pounds to their mother.'

Athens was full of the news. The mother took pains to consult lawyers, but none of them could explain how to arrange that the daughters should not have or enjoy what was given them, or how, if they gained nothing under the will, they could pay the money to their mother.

When the matter had dragged on for a long time and still no one could understand the meaning of the will, the mother gave up worrying about the legal position and decided to act according to her conscience. So she apportioned the property. To the coquette she assigned the clothing and woman's finery, the bathing equipment, and the eunuchs and pages. The industrious worker was to have the land and the herds, the farmhouse and labourers, the plough-oxen and pack-animals, and all the farm implements, while the thirsty wench was promised a cellar stocked with jars of vintage wines and an elegant mansion with a beautifully laid out garden.

When the woman was preparing to make over their portions to the girls amid general approval – for their characters were well known – Aesop suddenly appeared in the midst of the crowd. 'If their father knew what was happening,' he said, 'he would turn in his grave at the thought that the Athenians had so sadly failed to interpret his wishes.' Then, on being asked to explain, he solved the riddle which had puzzled everyone. 'Give the house and all its fittings,' he said, 'the beautiful garden, and the old wines, to the hard-working countrywoman; the clothing, pearls, foot-men, and the rest of it, to the bon vivant; the land and the byres and the flocks with their shepherds, to the coquette. They will not have the strength of mind to keep things that are alien to their characters. The ugly trollop will sell the finery to buy wine; the flirt will sacrifice her land to deck herself in rich attire; and the girl whose only interests are farm-stock and spinning will be impatient to get the mansion off her hands. So none of them will remain in possession of what is given her, and each can pay the prescribed sum to her mother from the proceeds of the sale of her property.'

¶ Thus, what had escaped a multitude of slow-witted men was discovered by the cleverness of one.

A CRAVEN BRAGGART

Two soldiers met a brigand. One fled, the other stood his ground and defended himself courageously. When the assailant was shaken off the coward came running up and drew his sword. 'Let me deal with him,' he said as he threw back his cloak. 'I'll show him what sort of men he has attacked.' 'I wish you had said that before,' replied the man who had fought it out. 'Even that much would have been a help to me; I should have felt more confident, because I should have thought you were speaking the truth. Now, sheathe your sword and hold your tongue – since the one is as useless as the other. You may be able to take in others, who do not know you. For myself, I have seen what energy you put into running away, and know how little trust can be put in your courage.'

¶ This story satirizes people who are brave while all goes well but take to their heels in time of peril.

NONE SO DEAF AS THOSE THAT
WON'T HEAR

Partiality often leads men into error: once they have made up their minds they stick obstinately to their mistaken opinion, and have cause to regret it when the true facts come to light.

A rich nobleman was going to give a public entertainment, and he offered a prize to anyone who could put on any sort of novelty. Professional entertainers were attracted by the hope of distinguishing themselves in this competition, and among the rest there came a jester, well known for his sallies of wit, who said he had a kind of show that had never been produced in any theatre. When the news got about, the whole town was excited (things happened to be very dull just then), and there were not enough seats for the crowd. When the jester took his place on the stage, without any properties or assistants, there was no need to call for silence; everyone was agog with expectation. Suddenly he bent his head into the fold of his cloak and imitated the squeaking of a piglet so cleverly that almost everyone said he had a real pig hidden in the cloak, and demanded that he should be searched. When nothing was found on him, many of them complimented him with presents of money collected on plates, and all applauded him as he left the stage. Among the spectators was a countryman. 'By God,' he said, 'he shan't get the better of me'; and without a moment's hesitation he undertook to beat the jester at his own game the next day. An even greater crowd collected then; for many people were so lost in admiration of the jester that they came just to make game of the countryman, not to see what he could do. The two competitors appeared on the stage, The jester grunted first – so convincingly that he won shouts of applause. Then it was the countryman's turn. He held his arms as if he had some object like a pig concealed in his clothes; but the audience, having discovered nothing when the other man was searched, thought it was only a pretence. In fact, there *was* a sucking-pig hidden there; and when the man pinched its ear, the pain naturally made it squeak. But the people said that the jester's imitation was much more like the real thing, and bundled the countryman head first off the stage. Whereupon he produced his little pig of flesh and blood – an undeniable proof of their disgraceful blunder. 'There!' he said. 'That shows what sort of judges you are.'

HIS OWN TRUMPETER

A man once read to Aesop some silly stuff that he had written, containing a lot of boastful talk about him, self, and he was anxious to know what the old man thought of it. 'I hope you don't think,' he said, 'that I am presumptuous or too cocksure of my ability.' The man's wretched trash made Aesop sick. 'I think you are quite right,' he said, 'to praise yourself. You will never find anyone to do it for you.'

FRAILTY, THY NAME IS WOMAN!

At Ephesus, many years ago, a woman who had lost a well-loved husband placed his body in a coffin, and nothing would induce her to tear herself from it. She lived continually in his tomb, mourning her loss, and by this example of chaste widowhood she gained high repute. One day some thieves who had robbed the temple of Zeus were punished for their sacrilege by crucifixion. To prevent anyone from removing their dead bodies, soldiers were placed on guard, near the tomb in which the woman had shut herself up. It happened one night that one of the soldiers was thirsty, and he begged a drink of water from the woman's slave-girl, who was attending her mistress as she retired to bed after sitting up late working by lamplight. The door stood a little ajar, and looking through it the soldier saw the widow. She was a fine figure of a woman and so beautiful that he fell passionately in love with her on the spot. As his desire gradually became uncontrollable, he applied his ingenuity to inventing innumerable pretexts for seeing her more often. These daily meetings made her more willing to yield to his advances, until at length her heart was enslaved. So it was with her that this watchful sentinel began spending his nights – with the result that a corpse disappeared from one of the crosses. In great consternation the man told his mistress what had happened. That model of wifely constancy was ready with her answer. 'There's no need to be afraid,' she

said – and gave him her husband's body to hang on
the cross, so that he might escape punishment for his
neglect of duty.

¶ By this foul deed the woman lost her former
good name and became a byword for iniquity.

BIG AND LITTLE FISH

Pulling his net ashore, a fisherman found a number of big fish caught in it and spread them out on the ground. But the smaller ones had escaped through the meshes into the sea.

❡ It is easy for people of moderate fortune to be safe, but you will rarely see a man of great note escape from peril.

FISHING IN TROUBLED WATERS

A man was fishing in a river. After stretching his nets right across the stream from one bank to the other, he tied a stone to a cord and beat the water with it to make the startled fish swim into the meshes without looking where they were going. One of the inhabitants of the place saw him and reproached him for muddying their clear drinking-water. 'But the stream has to be disturbed like this,' he answered, 'or I must die of hunger.'

¶ It is the same with nations. Agitators succeed best by stirring up strife.

FAMILIARITY BREEDS CONTEMPT

When men first set eyes on a camel they were terrified by its huge size and ran away. But in course of time they discovered what a gentle beast it was and plucked up courage enough to approach it. Gradually they came to realize that it was incapable of anger; then they despised it so much that they put a bridle on it and let their children drive it about.

¶ Formidable things lose their terrors when we get used to them.

SELF-DECEPTION

An amateur singer who hadn't a voice used to sing all day, accompanying himself on a lyre, in a house with plastered walls, which amplified the sound so much that he imagined himself to have a first-rate voice. His conceit made him think he was cut out for the stage. But when he appeared in public he sang so atrociously that he was chased off with a volley of stones.

¶ In the same way there are some would-be orators who in the schools pass for men of ability but are a complete failure when they enter public life.

¶ Notes

⁋ Notes

The letters and numbers indicate where the original text of each fable (not always the same version as the one here translated) can be found. C refers to Chambry's 'Budé' edition, H to Halm's edition, Hs to Hausrath's edition, P to Perry's edition, and Ph to Phaedrus. For details of these texts, see Introduction, page xxii.

1. C30; H31; P24; Hs24. Another version makes the fox enter a herdsman's hut to get at the food. Horace (*Epistles*, 1. 7. 29–33) has a version which makes it enter a corn bin. Richard Bentley was so outraged by this – since foxes do not eat corn – that he proposed to read *nitedula* (shrew-mouse) instead of *vulpecula*. But there are other fables which contradict facts of natural history.

2. C31; H32; P19; Hs19.

3. C32; H33; P15; Hs15a.

4. C34; H35; P22; Hs22.

5. C38; H44; P81; Hs83.

6. C39; H43; P14; Hs14.

7. C40; H45; P9; Hs9.

8. C41; H46; P17; Hs17.

9. C43; H47b; P27; Hs27.

10. C165; H204; P124; Hs126.

11. C196; H246; P142; Hs147.

12. C200; H247; P147; Hs152.

13. C209; H260; P149; Hs154.

14. C270; H326; P191; Hs203. In this fable the fox – for once – fails to see far enough ahead.

15. H36; P427; Aristotle, *Rhetoric*, 11. 20.

16. C59; H63; P284.

17. C194; H240; P257; Hs167. This is one of the shortest fables in the collection, but deservedly one of the most famous. The lioness's answer could not be more terse and apposite.

18. C198; H249; P140; Hs145.

19. C203; H253; P338.

20. C204; H254; P148; Hs153.

21. C207; H258; P339.

22. C210; H261; P259; Hs292. Prometheus ('The Forethinker') was a popular demi-god, supreme in trickery and in crafts-manship, who made men and animals out of clay. When Zeus took away from men the fire that they needed to practise handicrafts, Prometheus stole it and brought it back to earth.

23. Ph I. 21. By Phaedrus' time the moral has become such an essential part of the fable that he generally puts it at the begin-ning, although this seems less effective than to let the story speak for itself and then add the moral merely to sum up and drive home the lesson.

24. Ph II. I. Writing in a sophisticated age, when Satire became an important branch of literature at Rome, Phaedrus cannot refrain from pointing out how, in the real world, the meek are denied the reward they deserve.

25. H241; P450; Aristotle, *Politics*, III. 13.

26. C205; H255; P258; Hs269.

27. C216; H266; P342.

28. C221; H274b; P155; Hs160.

29. C224; H276; P156; Hs161.

30. C227; H279; P347.

31. C228; H281; P348.

32. C229; H283; P234; Hs165.

33. C313; H373; P209; Hs225.

34. C314; H374; P267; Hs276.

35. H280; P260.

36. H376; P451.

37. C191; H237b; P138; Hs143.

38. C327; H407; P224; Hs252.

39. C206; H256; P150; Hs155.

40. C237; H291; P165; Hs174.

41. C243; H297; P352. Horace's elaborate version of 'Town Mouse and Country Mouse' (*Satires*, II. 6. 79–117) shows what the skill of a literary artist can make out of a fable:

'Once upon a time, the story goes, a country mouse wel-comed to his poor hole a town-bred mouse, an old friend whom he had entertained before. He lived frugally and kept an anxious eye on his store of food; yet his careful soul could unbend to please a guest. You can imagine the scene. He was not the mouse to grudge a friend his hoarded peas and long grains of oats; he brought dried berries for him in his mouth and half-nibbled bits of bacon, hoping by this variety of fare to tempt the other's fastidious appetite. But his guest barely condescended to take a bite of each dainty, while the master of the house, leaving all the best food for him, stretched himself on a couch of fresh straw and dined off spelt and darnel. At length the townsman grew impatient. "What pleasure do you find, my friend," he asked, "in living a hard life on this steep wooded slope? Why not choose town and company in preference to rough woodland? Take my advice: come right away with me. Mortality is the lot of all earthly creatures; neither great nor small can escape death. So, my good sir, live while you may in the enjoyment of good things, and remember how short your life must be." The countryman was impressed by these remarks. Out of doors he jumped in an instant, and they did the whole journey in one stretch, hoping to creep inside the city walls under cover of darkness. Night had just reached the middle of its course when they set foot within a wealthy mansion, where scarlet coverings gleamed on ivory couches and baskets stood piled high with dishes left from yesterday's great banquet. The country guest was made to lie at full length on a crimson coverlet, while his host ran to and fro like a waiter with tunic girt up, serving course upon course, and played the part of a house-slave to the very life, taking a preliminary lick at every dish he brought. His friend lay back, congratulating himself on the improvement in his fortune and acting the delighted guest, when suddenly a loud slamming of the doors made them both jump off their sofas. From end to end of the dining-hall they scampered in alarm; then the great house echoed with the barking of watch-dogs till they were scared out of their wits. "This life is no use to me," said the visitor; "so I bid you good-bye. For my part, I will stay in my forest hole where I am safe from surprises, and appease my hunger with humble vetch."'

42. C66; H76; P44; Hs44.

43. C127; H77b; P314.
44. C201; H248b; P141; Hs146.
45. C244; H298.
46. Ph I. 24. Horace (*Satires*, 2. 3. 314–20) gives a version in which a calf crushes a family of young frogs with the exception of one. The survivor tells its mother about the huge beast that has squashed its brothers and sisters. The mother frog distends herself and asks, 'Was it as big as this?' – and so on, until the young one tells her that even if she bursts herself she will never equal the size of the calf.
47. C75; H85; P48; Hs48.
48. C326; H71b; P214; Hs234.
49. C304; H362; P203; Hs219.
50. C305; H363; P73; Hs75.
51. C307; H366; P218; Hs243.
52. C81; H96; P51; Hs51.
53. C82; H97; P176; Hs62.
54. C122; H153; P221; Hs248. The name Zeus means 'sky', and Zeus was originally a weather god, who had his seat on Mount Olympus and made rain-storms and thunder and lightning. But he had also another aspect – that of the supreme *pater familias*. On earth he was protector both of human families and of the larger family which is the state, together, with its king; on Olympus he ruled the divine family consisting of his own children (Aphrodite, Athena, Artemis, Apollo, Ares, and Dionysus) and his vassal gods and goddesses. Families and states being upheld by customs and rules, he was the special guardian of law and morals.
55. C289; H345; P197; Hs212. Cats – cherished and honoured as sacred animals throughout Egyptian history – were not commonly kept by the Greeks or Romans of classical times. Their mousers were generally animals of the weasel type.
56. C291; H347; P198; Hs213.
57. C331; H393; P216; Hs236.
58. Ph IV. 8.
59. C306; H365; P83; Hs85.
60. C105; H126; P75; Hs77.

61. C199; H243; P336. The point of the fox's final question is that the heart was often regarded by the ancients as being the seat of the intelligence.
62. C247; H303; P351; Hs275.
63. C102; H128; P74; Hs76.
64. C125; H154; P106; Hs108.
65. C351; H419; P230; Hs259.
66. C352; H420; P226; Hs254.
67. C3; H5; P1; Hs1.
68. C79; H92. P296.
69. C5; H8; P2; Hs2.
70. C160; H199; P126; Hs128.
71. C161; H201; P123; Hs125.
72. C162; H200b; P101; Hs103.
73. C8; H9; P4; Hs4.
74. C166; H205; P323. Apollo, born in the Aegean island of Delos, was the son of Zeus and Leto. He is represented as the ideal type of manly beauty, and was the patron of music, prophecy, medicine, and higher civilization generally; he also taught men archery and the care of herds. His oracular shrine at Delphi was the most famous in the Greek world. In later antiquity he was often identified with the sun-god.

Hermes was another son of Zeus, born strong and cunning. On the first day of his life he made a lyre out of the shell of a tortoise which he killed, stole Apollo's cattle, and denied it when charged with the theft. He acted as messenger of the gods and as the guide of dead men's souls to Hades. On earth he was the protector of merchants – and of thieves – and the bringer of luck.
75. C349; H417; P39; Hs39a.
76. C355; H423; P244; Hs261.
77. Ph 1. 26.
78. C136; H170; P396; Hs315.
79. H210; P325.
80. C174; H216; P233; Hs247.
81. C20; H21; P281; Hs266. The moral – a quotation from the *Epistle of James* (iv. 6) – was obviously added by a Christian scribe or reader.

82. C180; H225; P252; Hs268.
83. C158; H195; P122; Hs124.
84. C28; H29; P25; Hs25. As an ornithological term the Greek *alcyon* means a kingfisher. In the world of fable it is a bird which builds a nest floating on the sea, and charms wind and water into calm during the halcyon days in winter while its eggs are being hatched.
85. C282; P238; Hs209.
86. C301; H357; P201; Hs217.
87. C302; H358; P202; Hs218.
88. C285; H356; P265; Hs205.
89. C286; H342; P192; Hs206.
90. C141; H177; P181; Hs286.
91. C142; H178; P320.
92. C328; P269; Hs238.
93. C12; H14; P16; Hs16.
94. C13; H15; P79; Hs81.
95. C14; H16; P7; Hs7.
96. C76; H88; P50; Hs50. Aphrodite was the goddess of beauty, love, and fertility (including vegetative fertility). She was probably of Eastern origin and akin to oriental deities of fruitfulness such as the Phoenician Astarte. In Greek mythology she was a daughter of Zeus (though another legend represented her as born from the sea foam) and wife of Hephaestus the fire god. By the Trojan Anchises she became the mother of Aeneas. The Romans identified her with the Italian goddess Venus.
97. C332; H396b; P217; Hs242.
98. Ph II. 7.
99. C16; H18; P279.
100. C17; H12; P6; Hs6.
101. C107; H134; P97; Hs99.
102. C321; H382; P212; Hs232.
103. C208; H259; P151; Hs156.
104. C263; H320; P237; Hs200.
105. C264; H321; P183; Hs194.
106. C265; H322; P180; Hs191.

107. C266; H324; P182; Hs193.

108. C267; H336; P188; Hs199.

109. C279; H333; P358; Hs199.

110. C275; H331; P91; Hs93.

111. C281; H334b; P187; Hs198.

112. Ph I. 15. Probably an original composition of Phaedrus, intended as a political satire. Rome had recently had several changes of masters. Sejanus, the all-powerful favourite of the emperor Tiberius, was disgraced and killed in A.D. 31; Tiberius died in 37; his successor Caligula was assassinated in 41.

113. C80; H95; P52; Hs52.

114. C175; H217; P92; Hs94.

115. C178; H62; P328; Hs283.

116. C181; H223; P253; Hs265.

117. C184; H231; P134; Hs137.

118. C185; H233; P133; Hs136.

119. C186; H224; P332.

120. C187; H226; P132; Hs135.

121. C276; H332; P264; Hs295.

122. C312; H372; P206; Hs222.

123. C345; H413; P Syntipas 16; Hs333.

124. Ph I. 23.

125. H228; Lucian, *Adversus Indoctum*, 30.

126. H238; P331.

127. C94; H115; P85; Hs87.

128. C342; H409b; P223; Hs251.

129. C95; H116; P62; Hs73.

130. C4; H7; P3; Hs3.

131. C151; H187; P322; Hs319.

132. C335; H400; P241; Hs245. The cicada's 'voice' is produced by the vibration of drum-like structures on each side of the insect's abdomen. A concert performance by an orchestra of cicadas is audible at a distance of a quarter of a mile. Frequent references in ancient literature indicate that the Greeks regarded it as a pleasant sound, though modern writers have compared it to the noise made by grinding a steel blade.

133. C188; H234; P255; Hs267.

134. C189; H235; P137; Hs140.

135. C234; H287; P163; Hs172.

136. C240; H294; P166; Hs175.

137. C241; H295; P112; Hs114.

138. C336; H401; P373; Hs114.

139. C242; H296; P235; Hs176.

140. C101; H125; P304; Hs263.

141. C143; H179b; P70; Hs239.

142. C323; H384; P369. 'Amaranth' is an English form of the late Greek word *amarantos*, 'unfading'.

143. C73; H82; P46; Hs46.

144. C346; H414; P271; Hs297.

145. H380; P Syntipas 4; Hs330.

146. C159; H197; P130; Hs132. An elaborate version of 'The Belly and the Limbs' is put by Livy (2. 32. 9–11) into the mouth of a fictitious Roman called Menenius Agrippa, who is said to have used it to convince the plebeians of their error when they went on strike and refused to co-operate with the patricians (494 B.C.).

'There was once a time when the parts of the human body did not all agree together as they do now; in those days each pursued its own objects and spoke its own thoughts. All the various parts resented the fact that their diligent efforts and service supplied the belly with everything it wanted, while it (so they thought) sat idle in the midst of them, doing nothing but enjoy the pleasures which were provided for it. So they concerted a plan. The hands refused to convey food to the mouth, the mouth rejected everything offered to it, and the teeth would not chew anything. By venting their spite in this way and trying to subjugate the belly by starvation, they reduced themselves, and the whole body which they composed, to the last degree of emaciation. Thus it was clearly proved that the belly is no idler, but as useful a worker as the rest; for the food, when fully digested, makes the blood on which our life and strength depend, and it is distributed in due proportion to all the veins and so conveyed to every part of the body'.

147. C2; H2; P99; Hs101.
148. C48; H118; P306.
149. C57; P311.
150. C74; H83; P49; Hs49.
151. C108; H137; P88; Hs90. Hera was a pre-Hellenic goddess, incorporated into Greek religious mythology as the sister and wife of Zeus, with whom she was much given to quarrelling. She presided over the life of women and especially over marriage and childbirth. She figures, with Athena and Aphrodite, in the story of the judgement of Paris, whose award of the prize to Aphrodite caused Hera to become the inveterate enemy of Troy. The Romans identified her with the Italian goddess Juno.
152. C112; H141; P309.
153. C120; H150; P108; Hs110.
154. C123; H132; P312.
155. C124; H155; P100; Hs102. Athena – supposed to have been produced fully armed from the head of Zeus – was the patron goddess of Athens, but she had cults in many other places also and was probably worshipped, as their protectress, by the Bronze Age princes of Crete and Mycenae. She is always represented as carrying arms, and fights with or for her favourite heroes and cities. She was also a patroness of arts and crafts such as spinning, weaving, pottery, and metalwork. The Romans identified her with the Italian Minerva.

Mōmus is merely a literary personification of fault-finding, unconnected with religious cult. He is first mentioned, as one of the children of Night, by Hesiod (*Theogony*, 214).
156. C253; H308; P173; Hs183.
157. C261; H316; P174; Hs184.
158. C298; H354; P239; Hs214.
159. C322; H383; P240; Hs228.
160. C259; H314; P355.
161. C87; H107; P57; Hs57.
162. C88; H108; P246; Hs278.
163. C91; H112; P56; Hs56.
164. C214; H264; P152; Hs157.

165. C233; H286; P161; Hs170.
166. C246; H301; P66; Hs67.
167. C260; H315; P178; Hs188.
168. C296; H351; P200; Hs216.
169. Ph I. 14.
170. C53; H300; P30; Hs30.
171. C58; H61; P283.
172. C83; H98; P42; Hs42.
173. C86; H103; P53; Hs53.
174. C129; H159; P316. Heracles was not a god – though oc-casionaly worshipped as one (see No. 188). He was the most popular Greek hero, with an ordinary human name ('Hera's Glory'), and the legends concerning him may have grown up round a real man, perhaps a prince of Tiryns. He per-formed his famous series of twelve labours at the bidding of Eurystheus, king of the neighbouring city of Argos. Many other adventures are related of him, and he was reputed to possess superhuman strength and courage. Athena is made to call him brother in reference to a legend which made him a son of Zeus by Alcmēne, the wife of Amphitryon, a native of Argos or Mycenae who went to live at Thebes.
175. C303; H359; P266; Hs229.
176. C254; H311; P65; Hs66.
177. C256; H309; P67; Hs68.
178. C287; H343b; P87; Hs89.
179. C308; H367; P78; Hs80.
180. C344; H412; P225; Hs253.
181. C51; H203b; P33; Hs33.
182. C52; H56; P31; Hs31.
183. C54; H57; P37; Hs37.
184. C89; H110; P55; Hs55.
185. C93; H114; P326.
186. C96; H117; P63; Hs63. Dēmādēs was a prominent orator and diplomat in the second half of the fourth century B.C. Unlike his more famous contemporary Demosthenes, he con-sidered that it was in the interests of Athens to come to terms with Macedon, and he rendered her good service by obtain-

ing the best terms he could from Philip and Alexander.

Dēmētēr (the last two syllables of the name are simply the Greek word for 'mother') was a fertility goddess who presided over the fruits of the earth, especially corn. Her worship was associated with that of a 'Maiden' (*Kore*), often called Persephone, who in mythology is Demeter's daughter and is carried off by Hades the god of the dead. Both mother and daughter were worshipped in the famous mystery rites of Eleusis in Attica.

187. C114; H144b; P68; Hs69.

188. C130; H160; P111; Hs113.

189. C133; H168; P317. Plutus personifies wealth (especially agricultural prosperity: hence he was described as a son of Demeter). He was popularly supposed to be blind, because he so often gave riches to the undeserving. In Aristophanes' play *Plutus* he gets cured of his blindness, so that he can see where he is going and visit the right people.

Lethe, which means 'oblivion', was the name given to one of the rivers of the Underworld. When the spirits of the dead drank of its water they forgot all that had happened in the upper world.

190. C248; H304; P169; Hs179.

191. C249; H305; P170; Hs180.

192. C295; H349; P363; Hs279.

193. C297; H352; P211; Hs230.

194. C309; H368; P204; Hs220.

195. C311; H370; P207; Hs223.

196. C318; H353b; P210; Hs226.

197. C343; H410; P375; Hs282. The last sentence of the epilogue is a paraphrase of *Job*, i. 21: 'Naked came I out of my mother's womb, and naked shall I return thither.'

198. Ph III. 9. Socrates the Athenian (469–399 B.C.) devoted most of his life to inquiries into right conduct, which he was the first Greek thinker to study critically and methodically. By his 'Socratic' method of questioning, and by his rigorous examination of fundamental assumptions and definition of terms, he also made an important contribution to logic. An

ascetic by temperament and habit, he was a man of re-
markable courage and inflexible devotion to duty, and had
great personal charm and a lively sense of humour. How
much of Plato's philosophical doctrine should be directly
ascribed to Socrates is uncertain, but through Plato and
other disciples he certainly had a far-reaching influence on
Greek thought. He was put to death after conviction on
charges of religious unorthodoxy and perverting the minds of
young men.

199. Ph IV. 5.
200. Ph V. 2.
201. Ph V. 5.
202. Ph Appendix 7.
203. Ph Appendix 13.
204. C25; H26; P282.
205. C27; H25; P26; Hs26.
206. C148; H180; P195; Hs210.
207. C156; H193; P121; Hs123.

FOR THE BEST IN PAPERBACKS, LOOK FOR THE

In every corner of the world, on every subject under the sun, Penguin represents quality and variety – the very best in publishing today.

For complete information about books available from Penguin – including Puffins, Penguin Classics and Arkana – and how to order them, write to us at the appropriate address below. Please note that for copyright reasons the selection of books varies from country to country.

In the United Kingdom: Please write to *Dept E.P., Penguin Books Ltd, Harmondsworth, Middlesex, UB7 0DA.*

If you have any difficulty in obtaining a title, please send your order with the correct money, plus ten per cent for postage and packaging, to *PO Box No 11, West Drayton, Middlesex*

In the United States: Please write to *Dept BA, Penguin, 299 Murray Hill Parkway, East Rutherford, New Jersey 07073*

In Canada: Please write to *Penguin Books Canada Ltd, 2801 John Street, Markham, Ontario L3R 1B4*

In Australia: Please write to the *Marketing Department, Penguin Books Australia Ltd, P.O. Box 257, Ringwood, Victoria 3134*

In New Zealand: Please write to the *Marketing Department, Penguin Books (NZ) Ltd, Private Bag, Takapuna, Auckland 9*

In India: Please write to *Penguin Overseas Ltd, 706 Eros Apartments, 56 Nehru Place, New Delhi, 110019*

In the Netherlands: Please write to *Penguin Books Netherlands B.V., Postbus 195, NL–1380AD Weesp*

In West Germany: Please write to *Penguin Books Ltd, Friedrichstrasse 10–12, D–6000 Frankfurt/Main 1*

In Spain: Please write to *Alhambra Longman S.A., Fernandez de la Hoz 9, E–28010 Madrid*

In Italy: Please write to *Penguin Italia s.r.l., Via Como 4, I-20096 Pioltello (Milano)*

In France: Please write to *Penguin Books Ltd, 39 Rue de Montmorency, F-75003 Paris*

In Japan: Please write to *Longman Penguin Japan Co Ltd, Yamaguchi Building, 2–12–9 Kanda Jimbocho, Chiyoda-Ku, Tokyo 101*

FOR THE BEST IN PAPERBACKS, LOOK FOR THE

PENGUIN CLASSICS

Netochka Nezvanova Fyodor Dostoyevsky

Dostoyevsky's first book tells the story of 'Nameless Nobody' and introduces many of the themes and issues which will dominate his great masterpieces.

Selections from the Carmina Burana A verse translation by David Parlett

The famous songs from the *Carmina Burana* (made into an oratorio by Carl Orff) tell of lecherous monks and corrupt clerics, drinkers and gamblers, and the fleeting pleasures of youth.

Fear and Trembling Søren Kierkegaard

A profound meditation on the nature of faith and submission to God's will which examines with startling originality the story of Abraham and Isaac.

Selected Prose Charles Lamb

Lamb's famous essays (under the strange pseudonym of Elia) on anything and everything have long been celebrated for their apparently innocent charm; this major new edition allows readers to discover the darker and more interesting aspects of Lamb.

The Picture of Dorian Gray Oscar Wilde

Wilde's superb and macabre novella, one of his supreme works, is reprinted here with a masterly Introduction and valuable Notes by Peter Ackroyd.

A Treatise of Human Nature David Hume

A universally acknowledged masterpiece by 'the greatest of all British Philosophers' – A. J. Ayer

FOR THE BEST IN PAPERBACKS, LOOK FOR THE 🐧

PENGUIN CLASSICS

A Passage to India E. M. Forster

Centred on the unresolved mystery in the Marabar Caves, Forster's great work provides the definitive evocation of the British Raj.

The Republic Plato

The best-known of Plato's dialogues, *The Republic* is also one of the supreme masterpieces of Western philosophy whose influence cannot be overestimated.

The Life of Johnson James Boswell

Perhaps the finest 'life' ever written, Boswell's *Johnson* captures for all time one of the most colourful and talented figures in English literary history.

Remembrance of Things Past (3 volumes) Marcel Proust

This revised version by Terence Kilmartin of C. K. Scott Moncrieff's original translation has been universally acclaimed – available for the first time in paperback.

Metamorphoses Ovid

A golden treasury of myths and legends which has proved a major influence on Western literature.

A Nietzsche Reader Friedrich Nietzsche

A superb selection from all the major works of one of the greatest thinkers and writers in world literature, translated into clear, modern English.

FOR THE BEST IN PAPERBACKS, LOOK FOR THE 🐧

PENGUIN CLASSICS

Aeschylus	**The Oresteia**
	(Agamemnon/Choephori/Eumenides)
	Prometheus Bound/The Suppliants/Seven
	Against Thebes/The Persians
Aesop	**Fables**
Ammianus Marcellinus	**The Later Roman Empire (A.D. 353–378)**
Apollonius of Rhodes	**The Voyage of Argo**
Apuleius	**The Golden Ass**
Aristophanes	**The Knights/Peace/The Birds/The Assembly**
	Women/Wealth
	Lysistrata/The Acharnians/The Clouds/
	The Wasps/The Poet and the Women/The Frogs
Aristotle	**The Athenian Constitution**
	The Ethics
	The Politics
	De Anima
Arrian	**The Campaigns of Alexander**
Saint Augustine	**City of God**
	Confessions
Boethius	**The Consolation of Philosophy**
Caesar	**The Civil War**
	The Conquest of Gaul
Catullus	**Poems**
Cicero	**The Murder Trials**
	The Nature of the Gods
	On the Good Life
	Selected Letters
	Selected Political Speeches
	Selected Works
Euripides	**Alcestis/Iphigenia in Tauris/Hippolytus/The**
	Bacchae/Ion/The Women of Troy/Helen
	Medea/Hecabe/Electra/Heracles
	Orestes/The Children of Heracles/
	Andromache/The Suppliant Woman/
	The Phoenician Women/Iphigenia in Aulis

PENGUIN CLASSICS

Pliny	**The Letters of the Younger Pliny**
Plutarch	**The Age of Alexander (Nine Greek Lives)**
	The Fall of the Roman Republic (Six Lives)
	The Makers of Rome (Nine Lives)
	The Rise and Fall of Athens (Nine Greek Lives)
	On Sparta
Polybius	**The Rise of the Roman Empire**
Procopius	**The Secret History**
Propertius	**The Poems**
Quintus Curtius Rufus	**The History of Alexander**
Sallust	**The Jugurthine War and The Conspiracy of Cataline**
Seneca	**Four Tragedies and Octavia**
	Letters from a Stoic
Sophocles	**Electra/Women of Trachis/Philoctetes/Ajax**
	The Theban Plays (King Oedipus/Oedipus at Colonus/Antigone)
Suetonius	**The Twelve Caesars**
Tacitus	**The Agricola and The Germania**
	The Annals of Imperial Rome
	The Histories
Terence	**The Comedies (The Girl from Andros/The Self-Tormentor/The Eunuch/Phormio/The Mother-in-Law/The Brothers)**
Theaetitus	**Early Socratic Diologues (Euthydemus/Hippias Major/Hippias Minor/Lysis/Charmides/Laches/Ion)**
Thucydides	**The History of the Peloponnesian War**
Tibullus	**The Poems and The Tibullan Collection**
Virgil	**The Aeneid**
	The Eclogues
	The Georgics
Xenophon	**A History of My Times**
	The Persian Expedition